HEATHER BOYD

BESTSELLING AUTHOR

MISS MAYHEM ✦ BOOK 2

MISS GEORGE'S SECOND CHANCE

MISS MAYHEM SERIES

BOOK 1: MISS WATSON'S FIRST SCANDAL
BOOK 2: MISS GEORGE'S SECOND CHANCE
BOOK 3: MISS RADLEY'S THIRD DARE
BOOK 4: MISS MERTON'S LAST HOPE

MISS GEORGE'S SECOND CHANCE
Copyright © 2013 by Heather Boyd
Edited by Sandra Sookoo

Prologue

---◆---

June, 1814
Brighton Shoreline

Difficult situations required desperate measures. Imogen George--writer, spinster and pragmatist--steeled her heart to be as brutal as any heroine before her had ever been. "Have you sulked enough Mr. Watson?"

The man sitting on the dark Brighton shoreline surged to his feet and then faced her. "Hell's bells, what are you doing here?"

Imogen clenched her hands together to hide their trembling. Standing on the dark beach, waves crashing around them, made her meeting with her best friend's brother potentially romantic though she doubted it would be. "I have a proposition for you, Mr. Watson. Do sit down."

She limped forward, annoyed that her clumsiness at dinner earlier in the evening at his house had robbed her of her dignity. It was not every day she pursued a man for conversation, even when he was her best friends elder brother. She was taking quite a risk being here but it was within her power to improve their lot. Peter Watson may lack the good sense to detect and seize his only chance for security, but Imogen would not. She had a plan for her life and Mr. Peter Watson would suit her needs perfectly.

When she found the place she meant to sit, Mr. Watson remembered his manners and gallantly swept his coat from his shoulders and spread it on the ground so she might rest upon it. She was pleased to see that even while desperate, he did retain some good qualities. Her hopes for a smooth resolution soared.

"Where is your chaperone, Miss George?" Mr. Watson asked suddenly, squinting into the darkness toward the township where their respective homes lay.

With her eyesight as poor as it was, Imogen couldn't say for certain in which direction her reluctant chaperone, her brother Walter, stood, so she waved her hand airily in the direction she'd left him, hoping her companion would not notice or point out if she were utterly wrong. "Walter is over there. Never mind about him for the present. Do sit down so I may avoid suffering a pained neck from looking up at you."

As Mr. Watson sank to the ground nearby, a weary sigh left his lips. "I am sorry I tumbled you over earlier tonight, Miss George. You have no idea how sorry."

"I did say at the time not to concern yourself unduly." In truth, Imogen was often clumsy outside her home. The objects of her surroundings were less likely to jump out and trip her up if she stayed in familiar territory. Friends frequently moved their furniture and if she could see with any degree of certainty, she would never have stood in Peter's way to have been in danger. As it was, the world was a trifle fuzzy at times—tonight being one of those. "The collision was as much my fault as yours."

How did Mr. Watson take her presence she couldn't tell, but she was determined to press on regardless. There was no point beating about the bush when she judged speed was worth being somewhat more forward. She had a solution to offer Mr. Watson that would meet his immediate need and her future requirements. "Marry me."

Her mouth grew dry and she swallowed, preparing for his response.

At her side, Mr. Watson furiously rubbed his ear. When he lowered his hand and did not turn his head in her direction, she repeated her proposal in a louder voice. "I asked you to marry me, Mr. Watson. What do you have to say about that?"

"That's what I thought I heard," he muttered. "I don't need pity."

Imogen heaved a heavy sigh. It had been too much to hope that he would leap on her proposal and agree immediately. A long discussion was undoubtedly necessary to secure his agreement. "I know. And I'm not offering you a bit of it. You need money. Immediately, or you will lose your home and perhaps be forced to debtor's prison. Your sister's heart is in danger of breaking if such a calamity should come to pass. I can help get you out of your predicament with little effort on your part and none at all on mine. It is a perfect arrangement."

He dug a hole in the sand between them with his fingers. "Surely there is someone you fancy to marry rather than me?"

She bent a look at him that she hoped conveyed her skepticism. "At my age? Society has me placed firmly on the shelf. It really is very simple to understand my motives: I would like not to live out all my days under my brother's roof. However, I'd rather not strike out on my own in order to gain a measure of independence. Society is unforgiving to a woman who challenges the conventions of proper behavior."

Mr. Watson scowled fiercely. "Society is stupid. You could marry anyone you want. Any one of your brother's friends, in fact."

Dash it all. Mr. Watson was the most stubborn man she had ever met. Would he lose the shirt off his back before he accepted help? Perhaps she should forget this. But then again there was no one else she'd consider making this offer to. "A confectioner is always an option for marriage I suppose. I do like caramels."

Mr. Watson ceased digging. "Linus Radley would be interested."

Really, this was all too mortifying. Did she have to go as far as beg? She and Mr. Radley had nothing in common at all. "Oh for goodness sake. Am I discussing marriage with Mr. Radley? No, I am speaking to you, Mr. Watson."

"There is Hawke."

Imogen laughed. Abigail, Mr. Watson's sister and her dearest friend, had undoubtedly fallen head over heels for the reserved banker next door and Imogen wouldn't interfere where there was no chance of success. Judging by Mr. Hawke's besotted looks through dinner that night it was very likely that a proposal could be in the wind. But it hadn't happened yet and there was no telling how long the banker would dither over the matter. "Don't be so foolish. Mr. Hawke has other prey in sight. I couldn't turn his head if I tried. I've chosen you so just agree and be done with it, or do you have an heiress waiting in the wings?"

Mr. Watson hunched forward, hugging his arms about his knees. "What heiress would take me?"

Stubborn, and feeling very sorry for himself. Mr. Watson was trying her patience. If Imogen was prone to violence there were any number of scolds she could inflict on him. Yet, Peter Watson needed her help and she needed him too. "Well, there is one sitting at your side right now, perhaps not a great heiress, but one who is offering you her hand in marriage."

There was a long pause, and Imogen took a moment to adjust her position to accommodate her sore bottom while she waited on Mr. Watson to see sense.

After a time, Watson glanced her way. "How large is your fortune?"

At last. Sensible discussion. "Large enough to cover your debts, dower your sister when needed, and live comfortably for the rest of your life provided a reasonable economy of spending is maintained."

He glanced away. "You've known about my problems before tonight, haven't you? How did you find out?"

When she placed her hand on his arm, he tensed. "Don't be cross, but Abigail confided in me some time ago. Your sister has been very worried about you and sought reassurance from a friend who could keep a confidence."

"Does everyone know?"

"I doubt it. Abigail only told me and with Hawke you can be assured of complete discretion in financial matters. We would never betray a friend."

He turned toward her. "I still don't understand why you would do this."

As she met Mr. Watson's gaze her palms grew slick. Doubts crowded her mind. She believed a match between them would solve their respective problems. There would never be love but respect and companionship would be enough, at least for her. "Perhaps I like you, Mr. Watson. I have had years to observe your nature and find little wanting, except perhaps for a degree more care when gambling."

"And if I were to lose your fortune to gambling?"

That possibility brought a bitter taste to her mouth. If Mr. Watson gambled her fortune away they may never recover sufficiently to live a comfortable life ever again. She had always been careful with her funds and she had to be sure Mr. Watson did not think he could waste her money on frivolous pursuits. "I am not in the least as forgiving as your sister, sir." Imogen squared her shoulders. "If that were to happen, our money spent with no regard for the future, then you would have a wife to remind you of that fact for all the days of your life. Ask Walter sometime to describe my personality when I've been thwarted."

Watson barked out a laugh, and his rigid posture eased a touch. "He has on more than one occasion. I did pity him at the time."

At least he was under no illusions that she was the sort to stand aside while he ruined them. "Good. Then I'm sure you understand the conditions under which you would accept my hand in marriage. Your charm will not gainsay agreement or forgiveness in every situation."

He covered her hand with one of his. "And what would?"

Imogen jerked her hand back. "I offered my fortune for a comfortable life with a marriage, nothing else. You may fall in love with whoever you choose, just do not have the bad taste to flaunt the woman beneath my nose."

Imogen's heart raced. Limiting the terms of her offer was purely for self-preservation. A marriage begun under these conditions did not grant Peter Watson access to her person for the mystical pleasure the marriage bed was whispered to provide. He would have to expend some effort if he desired intimacies. Imogen would not make it as easy for him to share her bed as she was handing over her money. She did not find him unattractive. He had a handsome face and tendency to smile, except at this moment. A woman who aspired to a higher level of independence than most had to draw the line somewhere.

After a time, Peter stood and held out his hand. "It seems we have an agreement."

Chapter One

July, 1814
A week before the wedding...

The world tilted for Peter Watson in a way he'd never anticipated. "Are you absolutely certain I'm the rightful heir?"

His new brother-in-law, David Hawke, slapped his shoulder. "It's confirmed. Not only are you the heir, but you are the recipient of a sizeable fortune to go along with it. You are wealthy now Peter. Or I should say Sir Peter Watson. Congratulations my friend."

Peter gulped past the lump in his throat. He'd dreamed of this but never truly imagined he'd ever inherit a title or fortune from a cousin so little remembered he'd needed to comb through old letters to find mention of the name. He was, or would be very soon, a baronet. It was all a bit much to digest so quickly. "What do I do now?"

David smiled. "A trip to London and then to Hereford to visit your holdings. It should all be settled within a month. I took the liberty of investigating your London townhouse before we came down to tell you the news. A very proper set-up. Servants, a town carriage and even a few horses, although they might be a bit long in the tooth for prolonged riding. Your relation was an invalid up until he died so be prepared for a degree of shabbiness about the house in the beginning."

Peter nodded slowly. A comfortable life beckoned. He'd be able to hold his head up with pride at last. He met Abigail's gaze and saw her beaming smile. He shook his head. "It seems impossible."

"I can hardly believe my brother will be a baronet too, but I am so happy for you," she gushed. "We rushed down as soon as we could to tell you in person."

Abigail also hadn't been able to stand still since the moment they'd appeared at his door direct from London. He hadn't seen her so happy in years, well except for her wedding day, and the day Hawke had proposed. "Then London it is."

"Wait," she cautioned. "What about your wedding? You are to marry Imogen next week."

Peter scrubbed a hand through his hair while thinking the matter through. If he could settle his inheritance before he married Imogen then his conscience would be clear. He would rather be seen to marry because he wanted to than because he was the next best thing to a penniless beggar and desperate for funds. Imogen would marry *Sir* Peter Watson and become Lady Watson. He couldn't wait to see her face when he told her the good news. "I'll go see her now."

"Very good," Hawke gazed about him with a barely suppressed smile. "We can leave for London tomorrow, early, settle the issues of the inheritance, and return as soon as possible to have you leg shackled. The place could do with a woman's touch."

Abigail's mock punches to her husband's midsection were pathetically half-hearted at best. The small dog wedged under her arm yapped at her behavior.

Hawke slipped his arm around Abigail and quieted the dog. "We'll be at home all evening should you need us."

When they were gone, Peter hurried to make himself presentable enough to call on his future bride, taking a moment to smooth his hair and straighten his appearance. It had been an eventful afternoon, but the thought of seeing Imogen tied his stomach into greater knots. She'd always had that effect on him, except now they were to be married the sensations only intensified. She was to be his wife. Never mind their arrangement had never involved mention of intimacies. He was to be her husband. He was determined never to let her regret her generous offer. He would prove her faith in him however he could.

He took a deep breath to steady his nerves before he tapped on her door. Her butler welcomed him with a smile and led him toward the sitting room. Usually Imogen greeted him with a soft easy smile, but today her expression was wary, her eyes were hooded in shadows as she dipped into a curtsy, her mouth set in a grim line.

Puzzled by it, he moved toward her and kissed her hand when she held it out, the absolute limit of their personal interactions. Her tiny hand slipped from his too quickly, as it always did.

"Good afternoon, Sir Peter."

His head snapped up. "You've already heard."

Imogen's dark brows drew together causing frown lines to appear. "This is Brighton. News travels remarkably fast."

He chuckled and stepped back. "That it does. David has only just confirmed the details. A house in London and all that entails: a Hereford property and sufficient income to support us in greater comfort than we could ever want."

"I am very happy for you." She tipped her head to study him. "The title suits you already."

His heart swelled. Imogen did not dole out compliments she didn't mean. He had enough experience of her temperament before the proposal to know such a comment was heartfelt. "It will suit us both very well." When she sank into her chair again, Peter took the seat opposite. "There is one catch."

"You are leaving."

Her soft words caught him by surprise. How the devil could she know that? He'd only just decided he needed to go. Was that the cause of her odd mood today? "I am. David believes it can be all settled within a month. He feels the quicker it is done the better for all concerned."

When her smile didn't reach her eyes, hope flared. Would she miss him? Even if their arrangement had started out as a loveless affair, he longed to hear she would think of him every now and then while he was away, or even a touch more than that.

"David is an imminently practical man. I admire sensible decisions." She drew herself up straight. "Which is why I feel it best to release you from our engagement."

Peter laughed at her joke and it took a moment to realize Imogen did not laugh with him. Her expression was as somber as he'd ever seen it. Understanding was like a punch to the gut. She thought he was running away from their marriage. "That's not necessary. I still intend to honor our agreement and marry you. I'm just asking for the delay of a month while I settle my affairs. Once that's out of the way we can go on as we planned."

Her smile grew sad. "You don't need me, Peter. You'll be a baronet. A gentleman with money enough to have anything your heart desires including a woman with a far better pedigree and one who might never bring scandal to your door with her wild imaginings."

"Now wait just a moment."

She held up her hand to stop him. "Don't contradict me. A writer who would rather spend her days with only her imagination for company is not a suitable candidate to be Lady Watson. Indeed, there is no need for you to marry a woman you do not love and none at all to choose me for your wife. After all, we both know the nature of our arrangement. No hearts are broken by an end to it."

A wild, painful thudding began in his chest, rising to a dull throb. "Now see here."

"No, Peter. It is done." She stood and held out her hand. "I am very glad for you, but the life you are headed for has no room for me."

He surged to his feet and grasped her shoulders. It seemed vital that he hold onto what he had started with Imogen. "Of course it has. And I don't care if you continue to write your stories. You know full well that, despite my initial surprise, I'm your biggest fan and supporter. I'm proud of you. Just think of the life you could lead and the inspiration you could find when we meet new faces and situations."

Her hands rose to his chest and kept him at a distance. She met his gaze directly, hiding nothing of her certainty in her decision. "I have done all of that. My imagination is quite good, but it would be selfish of me to deny you the freedom to choose with your heart. Go to London, visit your estate in Hereford, and enjoy your good fortune. Who knows, you may even find a woman who could love you as you deserve."

Sharp humiliation stabbed his chest. It was no secret between them that their arrangement had been for practical purposes. She had offered him her fortune to save him from debtor's prison and he had meant to repay her by being the best husband he could be. Lust or love had not been part of their relationship, but Peter had never understood before now that Imogen had never intended to let him close.

He dropped his hands from her arms, appalled that he had secretly hoped for more from their marriage, a deeper connection with his future wife. While he'd been imaging how their life together would unfold, she had likely been planning nothing of the sort. Would she have spent the wedding night alone, writing more stories to publish under the alias K.D. Brahms? He studied her face and saw the sad but determined expression that lingered there. She didn't truly want a life with him. Damn, then why offer her fortune to save him in the first place? Had Abigail convinced her of the necessity and only now that Imogen had the flimsiest of excuses could she get out of it?

The idea of being a mistake, or being found wanting, wasn't a new sensation, but with Imogen involved, he took it to heart. Peter stepped away. "Perhaps you are correct."

"I am," she said briskly. "How soon will you go?"

Could she not bear the sight of him a moment longer than necessary? Thank heavens he'd learned of her lack of feeling before the wedding day was upon him. He'd been saved a life of misery while hoping to win her heart. He willed his raging pulse to slow, to hide how great his disappointment. He glanced outside to the ending Brighton day and wished he could travel miles away in an instant to escape this humiliation. But he still had to pack and wait on Hawke. Tomorrow, on the journey, would be soon enough to break the news to his sister and her husband that there was nothing for him to return to Brighton for. He drew himself up to his full height, determined not to appear as broken and pitiful as he was inside. "Tomorrow. Quite early, I suspect since Hawke is arranging the carriage. I don't believe I shall see you again."

There was a long pause before Imogen spoke. "I imagine not. Pleasant trip, Sir Peter."

And that was it. Peter was a free man.

He strode from her house without a backward glance and into the sun setting on a summer's day that couldn't hope to warm him. His heart, wherever it had taken refuge, was better off without Imogen George. He stepped inside his empty house, grateful that he didn't have to face his sister or her husband, and slammed the door behind him. He would not give in to self-pity and bitterness. It was better to leave with no illusions. A year from now he would be blissfully happy with another woman. One who couldn't wait to see him each and every day.

Chapter Two

------◆------

One year later …

Imogen stared at the pinprick of light held before her eye and willed it to come into sharper focus or grow to its fullest size. The flame wavered and then the world went dark again as the doctor's candle was extinguished. The scent of melted wax, strong coffee and tobacco wafted over her signaling the doctor had just exhaled heavily and had no clue what to do to help her.

Another day with no good news. Imogen had long accepted darkness was her fate. Only her brother searched for a cure that likely didn't exist.

"Are you in any pain, Miss George?"

The deep rumbling inquiry set her nerves on edge. The same question as dozens had asked before, dozens of times. There was no pain. No discomfort but the suffocating black void of her new and unwanted world. Could they not think of a new way to question a patient whose senses were reduced by the most important one? The tell-tale clunk of a small glass bottle being deposited on a side table sounded beside her and she struggled to keep her temper in check. "There's nothing. I've no need for potions either, so please return that bottle you set on the table to its proper place before you go. I refuse to take it."

A significant side effect of her loss of sight was her improved hearing so she overheard the doctor's whispered promise to her brother that the potion could cure her. What utter rubbish. Along with her loss of sight was her lack of patience with her fellow man, especially when they were trying to sell her brother some concoction that would make her sick to her stomach.

She smiled pleasantly as her brother led the charlatan away, turning aside his claims of efficaciousness with promises to consider it. At least Walter had gained a degree of sense in detecting the signs of a money making scheme when he saw one and no longer grasped for cures. When she could no longer hear their heavy tread in the hall beyond her bedchamber, she turned her face to the warmth granted by the sun shining through the window and basked in the light breeze stirring the air. Another perfect Brighton day. If only she could be a part of it.

Imogen quashed the wish immediately. She'd had long enough now to prepare for the loss of her sight and not to hope for things beyond her reach. For two years she'd struggled with failing vision and her writing until she accepted that she'd have to give it up completely. She couldn't see to write. She couldn't review the words she'd written to make sure it all made sense and was free of errors. In fact, she couldn't even write her own letters to her best friend Abigail who now lived in London most of the year. Walter had that unfortunate chore, though he never complained out loud about her frequent correspondence.

For a time, she'd considered hiring a secretary. Someone to record her stories and read them back to her and make corrections. She'd even got so far as to discuss the matter with her brother, but Walter had been afraid of her secret writing life being discovered and what that might do for her reputation, and his.

In the end she had to agree that the risk to the family's reputation was too great. She also conceded it might also be a trifle awkward to speak such bold words as she was accustomed to using in her writing before a complete stranger. Her writing was private. No one knew what she'd given up because only her brother, David Hawke and Abigail knew the truth. Of course, her former betrothed had been informed of the real source of her wealth when the marriage contracts had been drawn, but she'd not heard of him since the day she'd broken their engagement a year ago. She hoped he continued to keep her secret.

So, KD Brahms had retired from writing and Imogen George had retired from life. It was better this way, but not at all easy. Every now and then, she forgot she couldn't see and crashed into someone or something in her hurry to act. It was all rather embarrassing and had given her detractors ample amusement over the past months. That was why she preferred to remain at home.

She stood and reached for her walking stick, using it to guide her through the house and down the stairs. She'd fallen just last week due to a careless misplacement of a chair and she wasn't quite so confident when she moved around still. Guided by the number of steps she took, she moved to the sitting room, took a place beside the window on her favorite wide couch and waited for her brother's return. They always discussed the latest treatments presented by the fellows he brought to her. Today she was determined to make him stop his search for more.

She didn't have to wait long.

"You could have at least heard him out," Walter grumbled as he fell into the chair opposite with a great crash.

"What was the point? They all say the same thing. Bed rest, a daily sip of a potion so vile it should not be inhaled, and faith that I will see again. I'm tired of it all. Please don't bring another stranger home with you again."

She heard the heavy sigh and the creak of furniture as her brother shifted. "Very well. No more strangers."

Although that might sound like a promise, Imogen knew better than to believe her brother would give up entirely. He'd been all she could have hoped for. He even accepted why she had entered and ended her engagement to Peter Watson so quickly last summer without argument.

"Good." Imogen kicked off her shoes and tucked her feet beneath her. "Now, what are you doing for the rest of today? I hope you're not planning to loiter about in case you're needed again."

Walter's chair creaked. "I don't like to leave you all alone so much."

Imogen grinned. "I won't be alone today. Miss Radley sent a note 'round saying she was coming to call. No doubt she has juicy gossip after the ball last night so I should be well entertained."

"Good," Walter said. "As long as it's not Miss Merton coming to call with her. I will not have that woman in this house ever again."

Imogen sighed. "Really, brother. You must make allowances for petty ignorance. I blame Miss Merton's parents for her groundless fears. As if blindness was catching. Her elder brother is an enlightened man. Perhaps in time Merton can convince her I am not diseased."

In truth, Melanie Merton's ignorance had been a startling shock at first. Her former acquaintance would not even stand beside her now. Imogen was very glad not to see the expression on the woman's face anymore but she could hear the odd tremble in her voice from time to time when their paths crossed. Most days, she strove to ignore it.

"I thought she had a brain in her head," Walter said savagely. Walter could not seem to follow her example.

Imogen hated it when Walter became upset and searched for a way to change his mood. "Well, perhaps it was on holiday when she learned the news about my loss of sight. I forgave her a long time ago. Surely you can do the same."

A *humph* was all he managed.

Imogen held out her hand and her brother quickly took her small one in his. She squeezed. "Get along with you now and enjoy the day. Don't come home smelling like the bottom of a barrel. My sense of smell is very keen now."

He kissed her cheek. "Miss Merton's a fool but we've an invitation to dine with them tonight. Valentine believes that time will prove her fears groundless. I won't allow you to hide from her as if she is right."

Imogen shook her head. "Be sure to offer my apologies. Don't argue. You know you'll only lose."

Another deep grumbling sigh and Walter withdrew from the room with a reluctant farewell. He thudded around the entrance hall and then the front door opened and closed with a heavy crash. Imogen clenched her hands together, disappointment and resolve filling her. Dinner parties were utterly impossible. She didn't dine before others anymore as there had been too many messy accidents in the past, moments where nervous laughter was smothered but heard anyway as she accidentally scraped food onto the tablecloth or knocked over a wineglass. However, she did miss the lively conversation that often sprung up between her neighbors. They were such a complex range of characters, all playing out their lives with no idea she'd been studying their every sly look or indiscretion and basing the occasional character on their foibles.

She rested her head against the back of her chair and closed her eyes, trying to ignore the loud ticking of the clock while she sat doing nothing. In the past, these quiet moments alone with her thoughts had helped her solve problems in her story telling. But now that she could not write, her story ideas only tormented her with no hope of release.

A floorboard creaked, and even though she couldn't possibly see, she opened her eyes.

"Drat," a feminine voice muttered close by. "Still not quiet enough to get by you undetected."

"Honestly, Julia, that's not a nice trick to play on a blind woman." Imogen scowled but found her friend's attempts to fool her sweetly endearing. Julia Radley meant no harm and it gave them something else to talk about besides gossip. The exuberant young lady was the perfect distraction on a dull day.

"I'm testing your hearing," Julia warned her footfalls coming closer. "You claim it's superior now that your sight has deserted you, but you didn't notice my arrival over the noise of your brother's departure. You've a way to go before you can claim pre-eminence yet."

Imogen laughed and held out her hand. "How are you today?"

Julia took it before thumping onto the cushion at her side. "Oh, well enough." She wriggled around at Imogen's side and the sound of a twig snapping reached Imogen's ears. "How did that get there? Never mind. I definitely think I can make it out my window and scale the trellis in less than half a minute. I've done it twice already today."

Imogen raised an eyebrow. Julia enjoyed setting herself

impossible challenges. Her latest scheme was attempting to escape her house unnoticed and by any unconventional methods possible. Climbing out the window was new though. "In a gown?"

"Of course in a gown." There was a pause. "I did acquire a pair of Linus' old breeches before I made the attempt, adjusted so they would stay securely affixed to my waist and wore them underneath my gown."

Imogen pressed her hand to her chest in horror but laughed anyway. There was nothing Julia wouldn't do to escape being a complete lady. "A wise precaution. Suitably scandalous but at least if you fall and become entangled in the trellis there's not a chance of your rescuer seeing more than he should."

Julia tutted. "As if I'd need rescue."

She squeezed the hand she held, imagining Julia's indignant face. The only person who would need rescue would be the gentleman Julia set her heart on to marry. Her friend hadn't mentioned anyone for the past year, not since Imogen's own marital prospects had ended, but it was only a matter of time before the young woman singled out a handsome, dashingly romantic man she meant to sweep off his feet. "What shall we talk about today?"

"I have news." Julia grasped her hands tightly and shook them up and down in her excitement. "My challenge to race one of the boys has finally been accepted and the date is set. Tuesday at noon."

Dread filled Imogen as Julia paused, her breath rushed. A year ago, Julia had dared the gentlemen of the street to a swimming race in the ocean and been refused. At the time, no one had believed the challenge was worth the effort or the notoriety such a scandalous activity would bring down upon those involved. Imogen had hoped the matter had been forgotten. "Who accepted?"

"On that, I am sworn to secrecy until the very moment of our race though I am bursting to tell you every exciting detail. He threatened to change his mind if so much as a whisper of his name was heard. I'd be cross with him if the idea of beating him wasn't so appealing."

Imogen clutched Julia's hands. "Please think of the consequences. You may ruin your reputation so badly that no decent man would marry you."

Julia huffed softly. "Well, I wouldn't want to marry a man who thought my reputation ruined by a bit of harmless sport. For years now our brothers and their friends have lorded their sporting prowess over us and it is time to challenge them to prove it. Will you come or not? It would mean so much to me if you were there to see my triumph."

Imogen pulled her hand back into her lap. What she dreaded most was stumbling about in public. The constant worry that her escort would forget and desert her sent an uncontrollable panic through her every time she considered the chances. Walter wasn't always the most attentive brother. "You know I will not be able to see your victory."

Her hand was caught up again. "I know but please. It would mean so much to have a friendly face in the crowd. Come on, Imogen. You hardly ever leave the house. I will miss hearing your thoughts about the race and what you discover is said from the shoreline."

When Julia pressed a kiss to the back of her hand, Imogen's resolve to remain apart from society cracked. If Julia was prepared to resort to sweet kindness to get her way, which she usually avoided, Imogen may as well admit defeat before the poor girl embarrassed herself. Nothing stood in Julia's way when she had a goal in mind. "Very well. I'll do my best to be there. Now tell me the particulars so I can convince my brother to deliver me to the beach to watch. Or listen as in my case."

Julia quickly told Imogen the plan for the event without slipping out the tiniest detail of whom she was competing against. The girl knew how to keep a secret, but Imogen still worried. "Who knows," Julia continued, "you may catch the eye of a chivalrous gentleman and be swept off your feet by his attentiveness."

Although her fears for the event outweighed her own misgivings, Imogen had to laugh at her friend's unwavering support. Until her sight had been lost, she had never known truer friends than Abigail Watson and Julia Radley. Imogen caught

Julia's hand as tears filled her eyes. "Dearest Julia. You are such an optimist. How many times must we have this discussion? That part of my life is over. No man would marry a blind woman if he had a better choice."

"Maybe Sir Peter will come back and be moved by your situation."

Imogen shook her head sadly. Julia had never lost her faith that her one-time-betrothed would return to Brighton and be so distressed by her condition that he would immediately propose and swear his undying devotion. But Peter had moved up in the world and moved on with his charmed life. She hadn't seen or heard from him since she had ended their betrothal. Even Abigail did not write of him and she'd never dared ask. "I couldn't bear to be married now and I am certain Sir Peter has many more pressing concerns. I'm sure he's never given me a second thought."

No, Peter was happier as he was living a life full of fun and adventure. Her chest tightened with sadness. At least she hoped so. One of them deserved to see the world.

Chapter Three

Sunshine and the scent of the restless sea filled Peter's nostrils the moment he stepped from his hired carriage and looked along Cavendish Place. Despite the improvement in his situation, his fortune and title of baronet, it was good to be home again among familiar sights and sounds of Brighton.

London for all its amusements wasn't where his heart longed to be. He'd tried to carve a place in society and had never found contentment. The most enjoyment he'd found was discussing books with the proprietors in London's bookshops.

He smiled at the memory. The booksellers were astounded he was acquainted with the author K.D. Brahms. He'd dodged any questions that might accidentally reveal the author was a woman—one whom he'd almost married—and discussed the lack of the next volume. There hadn't been a new story published in a year and he, along with everyone else in society, was keen to find out when the next could be delivered. Surely Imogen would tell him if he asked nicely. There had to be some advantage to keeping her writing life a closely guarded secret.

He looked along the street, noticing more than one head pressing to the window glass. Friends waved and promptly disappeared again, giving Peter the hope he'd see them shortly. He wanted to see all his neighbors, too. Even the pretty, dark-haired petite one who had rejected the idea of marrying him the moment his financial future was assured. Surely there was no need for them to be strangers to each other.

The door to his abode wrenched open and his servants, Mr. and Mrs. Simpson, stood gaping at him. "Why didn't you say you were coming, sir?" Mrs. Simpson wailed the complaint, wiping her hands on her spotless apron. "I'm not ready."

"Not ready to serve my favorite beef stew and dumplings with lemon pudding to sweeten my palate?" He grinned at his housekeeper. "Come now. I'm not falling for that."

He shook their hands, very glad to see them looking well and happy, and stepped aside as the hired carriage grooms tramped inside with his possessions. He pressed coins into the grooms' hands. "The Rose and Crown will serve you well if you're to stay overnight. Try to stay out of trouble. The proprietor is a good man and a friend."

"Thank you, sir." They grinned and returned to the carriage, leaving Peter to his own devices. He stepped across the threshold and breathed a sigh of relief. Home. No invitations to stuffy balls, no simpering debutants to be agreeable with, and far less rules to follow. He couldn't believe he'd stayed away so long.

Nothing had changed in the house and that was exactly how he liked it.

"Where the devil have you been?"

He spun about to find Valentine Merton, grinning face and all, hovering in the open doorway. "Everywhere and nowhere. Come in. Come in and have a drink with a weary traveler."

"You don't look too battered by your adventures." Merton peered at him carefully as he stepped inside. "In fact, I wondered about your extended absence. For a while there I thought you might be too good for us now you've a title. Took you long enough to visit."

Peter narrowed his gaze. "What a ridiculous thing to suggest that I am merely visiting. I had a few matters to attend to in London and Hereford. That's taken care of now."

"Good." Merton grinned and looked around him. "It's dinner at my house tonight and cards tomorrow evening, here in fact. Is that notice enough, Sir Peter?"

Peter threw a mock punch at Merton and gestured toward the

dining room where he usually met with his friends. "More than sufficient and actually will make my housekeeper very happy. In my eagerness to return, I neglected to forward prior warning so she could prepare dinner for this evening. Tell me, who else will be there?"

"The usual crowd. All but Hawke and your sister, but at least he writes to say when to expect him. I think that's your sister's influence."

Peter rubbed his jaw as he inspected the rear of his property through the casement window. He smiled at how everything appeared as he'd left it a year ago. The kitchen garden was flourishing this year. "She has made an impression on him. I've never seen him smile so much."

"I noticed that, too, the last time they came down."

Peter spun about to face his guest. "That smile appeared at the moment they decided to marry and hasn't faded once, no matter what happens or how busy he gets with work."

"Thank God for Abigail." Merton made himself comfortable. "I really did fear Hawke's heart was growing as cold as the money he counted."

"No chance of that now." Peter reached for the brandy, poured a measure for his friend and one for himself. He'd been so wrong about Hawke and his sister. They were very much in love. "My sister would never stand for it."

Another knock sounded on the door, and Peter hurried into the hall again. Linus Radley stood cap in hand, a hesitant smile on his face beside Simpson. "Good afternoon, Sir Peter. Thought I should come pay my respects early before the whole town arrives."

"You're late. Merton beat you to it. Come in, come in. We're about to have a brandy." He led Radley into the dining room and poured another drink.

When he turned, Merton looked him over curiously. "So, do tell. I'll be the blunt one to ask the question burning on everyone's lips. How big is your estate?"

Peter passed out the glasses and took a sip before answering. "I sold the country estate actually."

Radley's eyes widened. "You what?"

Peter shrugged. "Can you imagine me running around chasing cattle and geese?"

Radley shook his head. "But you had property."

"One that didn't suit me or my preference for life near the sea." Peter took another drink. "I sold it for a pretty penny though thanks to Hawke's sharp negotiations and purchased something else a little closer to home. Or rather a few little something's."

When his friends appeared puzzled he clarified, enjoying the expressions of surprise on their faces. "I bought the old Trent place on the hill overlooking Brighton, not that I intend to live there, as well as another smaller property for the additional income."

Merton's eyebrow rose. "So this house is what you mean by home?"

"Of course." He leaned back in his chair, content at last. "It's taken me a year to straighten it all out. The estate sold to a neighbor who'd coveted the Herford property for some time. Hawke and Abigail have moved into the London townhouse. I couldn't see the sense in leaving it empty most of the year and Abigail and that mutt of hers have taken it over completely."

"And you're back now to lord your title over us all," Merton teased.

"Hardly. I'm home to stay so I don't intend to put on airs and be laughed at every other moment." Peter rubbed his hands together. "It'll be like old times."

Merton and Radley exchanged a long look. "Well, that's good to hear. Radley, we should go and let Sir Peter get settled. Dinner is at eight o'clock. Be prepared to have your ears talked off and be questioned unmercifully."

Peter grinned. "I look forward to it." He couldn't wait to hear the local news. It was amazing how much he'd missed everyone's chatter. Discovering news third-hand, through Abigail's letters and confidences, had not been enough.

Peter walked his guests to the door, as he would have done before he'd gained a title, looking beyond them down the familiar street he'd spent his whole life strolling along. His gaze narrowed as Walter George, his nearest neighbor, stopped on his front steps with a distinguished looking gentleman at his side. The man was a touch taller than Walter, of similar age and carried a wrapped parcel in his hands.

Walter paused, a frown working over his features and then touched the brim of his hat. He made no move to join them and they disappeared inside his townhouse.

Peter glanced at Merton and Radley. "What was that about?"

"Perhaps it has something to do with Miss George." Radley shook his head, lips turning into an unhappy frown. "George is determined to see this through for his sister's sake."

An uneasy sensation stirred within him. "Has Miss George become engaged again?"

"No, of course not engaged." Merton exchanged a speaking glance with Radley. "I don't believe he knows."

"Damnation." Radley settled his hat on his head. "If you don't mind, I think it best if I leave it to you, Merton. You know more about the matter than me. I'll talk with you later, Sir Peter, if you're still of a mind to come to dinner after all."

He strode off as Merton steered Peter into the house. All sorts of panicked thoughts filled his mind. Was she ill? Injured? Married and with child? Why did he see pity brimming in Valentine's eyes?

Merton shut the front door behind them, waved off his servants, and drew Peter toward the dining room again. A full glass of brandy was pressed into his hand. "Imogen is well but there has been a change in her prospects. For the worst, I'm afraid."

"Did she lose her fortune?" Peter looked toward the door, ready to render whatever assistance he could. He would offer to marry her in a heartbeat, to show her the same kindness she'd bestowed on him a year ago, to ensure her future comfort was always secure. He could afford to do so much for her now.

"No. It's far worse." Merton raked a hand through his hair. "There's no easy way to say it so I'll be blunt. Imogen George is blind."

It took a moment for the words to sink in and when they did Peter sank into a chair because his legs no longer felt strong enough.

Chapter Four

Imogen heard the heavy tread of her brother and frowned at the noise. The downstairs clock had just chimed eight and yet he was still pacing through the house. She felt for her walking stick and got to her feet carefully. If he was going to dine at the Merton's tonight he really should be gone already.

Determined to remind him of his obligations, she clattered into the hall and carefully descended to the lower floor one careful step at a time. At the foot of the staircase, she paused to get her bearings. Walter was pacing his study. She moved in that direction, catching the doorframe with her free hand and addressed the room. "Are you not late for the Merton dinner?"

"I changed my mind and offered my apologies to Merton. I'll dine at home tonight."

Papers shuffled and she moved further into the room. "Why change your mind? You know I do no mind dining alone. In fact, I find it preferable."

"You're not that bad anymore."

"Certainly not since Cook elected to serve me every meal with a consistency I can eat with a spoon." She sighed. "Cook has a practical turn of mind that I whole heartedly approve of."

"Nevertheless, we'll dine together as we should."

Walter's unfailing support brought a grin to her face. "As you wish. I'll see Mrs. Perkins and ask her to serve us now if you don't mind. You must be hungry."

"Thank you," Walter murmured.

With the aid of her walking stick Imogen navigated her way toward the kitchen. The scent of beef stew reached her first, then the added warmth of the lit stove on a hot summer's day. She paused at the doorway, sensible of the dangers that lurked inside a busy kitchen. Mrs. Perkins was involved in her tasks and Imogen should not proceed any further for fear of accidentally getting in her way. She'd bumped into a heated pot once, burning the edge of her hand and feared further misadventures that would cause similar or worse pain.

"Good evening," she said to the room as a chair scraped across the floor. "The stew smells divine and has set my stomach to rumbling. May we eat soon please? Walter is joining me rather than going out and you know how he is about late meals."

"Yes, the master warned me earlier he would be at home tonight," Mrs. Perkins said. "I'll be along to the dining room presently."

Without her aid and advice during these troubling times, Imogen would have wallowed in maudlin thoughts long ago. "Thank you."

Imogen pushed away from the door, held her walking stick before her, ready to venture to the dining room and wait. But as she did so she heard a soft feminine sob come from the room behind her. Since the servants had ceased crying over Imogen's blindness many months ago she frowned at the strangeness of it and turned her face toward the kitchen. "Is someone with you?"

Mrs. Perkins rushed to her side and caught her elbow. "No, my dear. I've just a touch of the sniffles tonight."

The comforting touch of the older woman's hand caused her to relax as she was led along the short hall. Though she would never deny her servants visitors, Imogen hated being secretly observed in her own home. Early on in her illness she had laid down the rules to Mrs. Perkins about strangers in the house. They were to be announced to her so she was not surprised by their presence. She must have imagined the sensation of another. "Make sure to take your own medicine tonight. I'd hate to have you fall ill."

Mrs. Perkins patted her hand. "You're kind to worry about me. I will look after myself perfectly well. Don't fret on my account."

Imogen couldn't help but fret. There was nothing else she *could* do. She moved off carefully, turned into the dining room and found her usual chair then sat. Being blind made one a touch desperate about the health and wellbeing of those around her. She trusted Mrs. Perkins and Mr. Perkins too and wouldn't like to have to train strangers to take over her duties if they should leave them.

"What has set you in a bad mood?" Walter stalked into the room and dragged out a chair. It creaked a little as he sat and his sigh was filled with annoyance. "You're frowning."

"Me? Nothing." She smiled quickly to reassure him. Walter became annoyed when she fussed about the servant's health and happiness. "I am hungry though so perhaps that is the reason for the frown you imagined."

The housekeeper's and butler's footsteps approached and she inhaled deeply of the scents of tonight's meal. The butler served her, efficiently silent, and departed, which was always appreciated. It made Imogen feel less like an invalid if there were fewer about to watch her clumsy attempts to dine.

She spread her fingers over the array of silver cutlery and chose a spoon. With her other hand, she located her bowl shaped plate. One best suited to her limited abilities to successfully load the spoon and avoid accidents.

Walter ate in silence a few minutes and then his cutlery clattered against his plate. "Are you happy, Imogen?"

"Of course I am."

"Really truly happy with things as they are? You would not lie to me about this, would you?"

"Yes, really truly happy." Imogen set her spoon upon her plate and although she turned in her brother's direction she found no great comfort from doing so. "What has brought on your questions, Walter? You're not considering searching for another physician to apply his dubious healing skills upon me. I could not have been clearer this afternoon. The next man you bring to examine me will feel the crack of my walking stick against their skull."

"No. I see you've made up your mind to give up on getting better."

"I am doing the only thing I can. I am blind. There is no getting around that fact. I could pitch about and moan about the unfairness of my life or accept it." Imogen stretched for him and was rewarded by his larger hand covering hers. "Or is it you who is unhappy with the prospect of my living with you for the rest of my life?"

"Of course not," he spluttered. "I only want what's best for you."

"And I you, which is why this might be the perfect time to discuss a solution." She took a deep breath and squared her shoulders. Hard decisions were always best handled with direct speech and no delay. "I've been considering my situation since I first lost my vision. I am a burden on you, Walter, and I will be a nuisance to the lady you will marry one day."

"There is no one, that is to say, I have no plans to marry as yet."

Walter would never have time to pursue a bride if he was always looking after her. He likely didn't even realize the full extent of the burden her lack of sight placed on him. "But at some time you will wish to have a family of your own, a lady to love and spend time with, and well, to be blunt, I doubt any woman would want to share a house with me. They would come to regard me as a burden and I do not ever wish to be that to your happiness."

"You're not a burden." He gasped. "Don't ever think that."

She patted Walter's hand and drew back. "I should like you to write to Hawke and arrange for the purchase of a small house with my fortune. Once that is settled, I will ask your help in interviewing a companion to care for me in my new abode. With your aid, and perhaps the assistance of a few discerning friends, and the Perkins' of course, I am sure I can be perfectly content."

"You're not leaving my house and my protection," he growled out, startling her with the tone of his voice.

Regardless of his intentions, she would have her way in the end. "That decision is not yours to make. Would you rather I walk out that door under my own steam, with no one to guide me away from trouble or catastrophe? If you help, you may be easy with the situation. Of course, you would be welcome to come for a visit at any time."

The chair Walter sat in gave a groan, as if he had rocked back on only two of the legs. "And have you planned where this little cottage of yours will be located?"

"I remember Fulking being very pleasant and quiet for an invalid."

"No. That's too far away." His chair scraped and his steps were loud as he paced the room. "I won't consider it and cease referring to yourself as an invalid. The whole notion is entirely unacceptable. You would never see your friends often enough."

"Walter, please. You must understand how difficult it is to live half a life when everyone around you is in the thick of it." She turned in her chair and hoped she faced him. "Miss Radley has begged me to watch her challenge some fellow in a swimming race. It is beyond ridiculous. I won't be able to see her triumph or fail. I spend my days with only my imagination to keep me company. I cannot embroider, I cannot make house calls, I cannot write or do the things most ladies take for granted. The torture of inactivity, of uselessness, with endless hours staring into the darkness is intense. What else is there for me to do with myself?"

"You used to play the pianoforte very well."

"When I was nine. I gave it up and wrote when I should have been practicing. I'm enough of a burden as I am without assaulting your ears by trying to learn again." Imogen threw her napkin on the table when she heard the clink of glass against the decanter. "Were you going to pour your blind sister a glass as well or just get foxed on your own?"

"You heard that?"

"Blind not stupid." Imogen sighed and stood, her appetite gone. "I hear far too much and not all of it good. Every whisper and snicker is mine to cherish in the dark hours of my life. Excuse me. I rather wish you'd left me to my own company tonight."

She fumbled for her walking stick and left the room with her head high and as much dignity as she could muster. She was a burden to her brother's life but he just would not say so. In time, he'd see that she was right to leave.

Chapter Five

They often said that maintaining a polite mask of indifference in difficult circumstances was a sign of a true gentleman. Whoever said so was mad. Peter's ability to maintain that mask was sorely tested after the shocking news he'd heard today about Imogen George. Discovering his former fiancée was in so terrible a situation had threatened his calm. Peter schooled his features to blankness as he stepped into the drawing room of Valentine Merton's modest townhouse and looked about at the assembled guests, even while his heart ached with sadness.

The ladies he'd grown up beside curtsied to him as if he were someone other than himself. Luckily, his male friends had seen sense and left off ridiculous excess in their greetings. They treated him as he wanted to be. A part of a life he'd been absent from at the worst possible time. He scanned the room for Imogen but could not see her or her brother yet. There was one lady across the room he didn't recognize at first but her slender form tugged his memory until her identity came to him. The vicar's daughter. Another chatterbox if he recalled correctly. Hell, he hoped he was spared her company at dinner.

The first of his friend's family to reach him was Miss Melanie Merton, an often shrill and unforgiving woman. Today her smiles were friendly, and not for one moment did he believe them to be anything but calculated to curry favor. In the past, Melanie had been far too open in her dislike for him and the fact that he was not rich. He was now, and that likely accounted for her pleased smile at seeing him.

"So good of you to come and grace our home with your presence, Sir Peter," she gushed. Her eyelashes fluttered as she continued smiling at him and he almost laughed at her transparent reversal of attitude. Did she think he wouldn't remember her true nature? He wasn't forgetful in the least and he did not easily forgive the slights she'd directed toward his sister before Abigail's marriage.

"Miss Merton. A pleasure to see you again," he told her, although he could have gone many days without. He glanced past her as Valentine Merton gestured Peter to come toward him. "Excuse me."

He stepped around her but was stopped again by the presence of Miss Teresa Long, his host's sweeter-natured cousin, blocking his path. He smiled sincerely. "You're looking very well, Miss Long. So good to see you again."

Peter had always made a point of praising Miss Long and just because he was a baronet he had no reason to cease their harmless flirtation. Her cousin Melanie Merton was far too happy to offer all too many subtle snubs and their infrequent talks always seemed to lift Miss Long's spirits.

Miss Long smiled warmly, her posture changing to one with greater confidence. "Thank you, sir. I must say, you look rather dashing tonight as well."

Her compliment, while sincerely offered, meant nothing beyond the friendly banter it was meant to be. "Thank you," he replied.

Miss Long gestured to the slightly built lady lingering in her shadow. "Are you acquainted with Miss Jane Pease? She is the daughter of our vicar, Mr. Pease, if you recall and has recently come out in society."

When he bowed over her outstretched hand, the frail creature dipped a curtsy and smiled up at him in transparent joy. "So happy to make your acquaintance, Sir Peter. My father was pleased to hear of your return today."

Was he now? Peter couldn't fathom why. The vicar had cast many a sour look in his direction on Sunday mornings during services until he'd quit the district a year ago. The only thing to account for Mr. Pease's sudden happiness was that Peter was titled and rich, and the vicar had a daughter to marry off.

Peter sneezed suddenly. His eyes watered and as he inhaled, he became aware of the scent of lilac lingering heavily in the air between them. He hastily dug for a handkerchief and apologized.

Miss Pease touched his arm. "I do hope you're not in poor health, Sir Peter."

"No. No. I'm sure it's nothing." Peter sneezed again, certain now that Miss Pease's scent was the trigger for his reaction. A year of dodging traps and snares laid by wily debutants in London had prepared him for heightened local interest, but his response to the scent of lilac gave him the perfect excuse to move away. He bowed to her again and dabbed at his eyes. "Excuse me, there must be a scent in the air that disagrees with me."

Before Miss Pease could delay him, he slipped around her toward safer territory and an open doorway. Miss Julia Radley, a firm friend of his sister, stood in the path of the light breeze blowing in from the sea. She grinned from ear to ear and when he joined her, Miss Radley quickly curled her arm through his, leading him out into the night just a few steps. With fresh air in his overwhelmed senses, he quickly recovered his composure. He was grateful of the lifeline but then he grew aware of what he'd unwittingly done. He glanced back into the room anxiously. Luckily, they were in full view of all and in no danger of being considered alone. He did not wish to marry Miss Radley. No sane man would. The girl was exhausting.

Miss Radley shook her head. "She's not here. I doubt she'll come if you're looking for who I think you're looking for."

He glanced down at the cheeky sprite on his arm in alarm. "Am I looking for someone?"

"I think you were from the moment you joined us. It's in the way you scanned the room and couldn't wait to leave the others behind. I knew you wouldn't turn your back on her as others have done." She patted his arm. "The perfume Miss Pease doused herself in tonight merely gave you the perfect escape from her clutches. My brother had the very same reaction earlier. I overheard Miss Merton reassure Miss Pease that the scent was utterly delightful. Devious of her indeed. Be mindful or one of them will catch you."

Peter glanced inside again and his gaze settled on Miss Merton and Miss Pease while they engaged in whispered conversation. Miss Merton paused, turned her head toward him and her smile brightened as if she'd discovered a rare jewel. Peter shuddered. "Hmm, that is an unfortunate development. Miss Pease could do with a friend who would tell her the truth. I didn't come home to find a bride."

Miss Radley peered at him. "Are you married then?"

"Good God, no. Why ever would you think that?" He held up his hand. "No never mind answering. You're too much like Abigail for me to not remember how you all think. A man must be married, yes?"

For an answer, Miss Radley merely laughed.

"Before I forget, would you by chance be at home tomorrow? I ask because my sister sent some additional parcels to Brighton with me. She said it's rather urgent but the contents have to be kept private from everyone. I've no idea what that entails so I hope you understand. If nothing else, my calling on you first may thwart whatever plans and hopes are being hatched over there."

Miss Julia clutched his arm tightly. "Oh, I cannot wait until tomorrow. Abigail is so sweet to have remembered my request. I cannot wait until I can show Imogen or maybe I should not. She's always fretting over the things that matter to me."

Miss Merton joined them. "Showing Miss George anything is an exercise in futility. Even when she could see she lacked that certain panache in her mode of dress to truly stand out from the crowd." As Miss Merton delivered her put down, she fanned herself with the languid air of someone who was sure of her place and her right to say whatever she liked. She may be in her own home, but Peter's blood boiled. How dare she say such a thing?

However, she was his friend's sister. He couldn't say exactly what he pleased without consequences. He forced a tight smile to his lips. "Unlike some, Miss Watson has no need for the expense of a London modiste to make herself presentable. I've always thought her natural beauty was without artifice or design." He examined Miss Merton's fussy gown and artfully arranged hair with as mocking a stare as he could manage. How many hours had she spent primping before her looking glass?

Miss Merton pinked slightly and looked beyond his shoulder as if he hadn't just insulted her. "Dinner should be announced soon. Excuse me while I tend to my brother's guests. A hostess must *see* to everyone's needs."

Peter did not miss her one last dig at Imogen's sightless state. He cursed softly, but then caught Julia's open-mouthed stare. He quickly apologized for his poor choice of words.

"I am so pleased to see you haven't become entirely top-lofty." Miss Julia smiled as a blush climbed her cheeks. "Is it wrong that I don't disagree with your sentiments?"

He smiled at her honestly. "Not even a little in my opinion, but let's keep that a secret between us."

Recovered sufficiently from his sneezing fit, Peter stepped back inside, accepted a glass of wine from a servant, downed it, and then wished for another. He might need reinforcement to make it through to the end of the meal.

When they went into dinner, Peter was forced to sit at Miss Merton's side and endured even more subtle jabs at Miss George's expense. He couldn't imagine why Walter George had failed to attend but he didn't blame him one bit if this was the usual dinner conversation. From a disparaging remark he overheard, Walter George had changed his mind at the last minute.

Despite the annoyance of Miss Merton's company, he did glean more information from her conversation to cause him further alarm. The loss of a woman's sight was a huge blow to her status and prospects for a fulfilling life she assured him. As an unmarried woman with hopes of one day making a match, her chances for future security would be greatly reduced. Miss Merton heartlessly confided that Imogen George would never marry, despite her fortune, and that 'poor Mr. George' would be saddled with an unwanted burden.

Imogen could never be a burden. Some lucky man would fall in love with her easily if given half a chance. The idea of her married, and it was not the first time the thought had crossed his mind, didn't appeal. It never had. Peter applied himself to the meal laid out before him and made small talk, but he lapped up every single mention of Imogen George—the woman who would never *see* him again.

Chapter Six

Imogen stretched her senses as far as she was able but detected nothing except the quiet night of Brighton beyond the black of her vision. Walter had long since retired for the night oddly quiet of chatter and not in the least willing to consider her suggestion of moving to a less populated location. She should not have lost her temper with him. Her blindness wasn't his fault nor was there anything he could do to improve her situation. She bit her lip. Her decision was the only sensible future she could imagine for both of them.

She eased her way down another step, aware that her brother would splutter and bluster should he discover her outside and alone like this. But he was fast asleep in his bed, muttering to himself in his dreams. Until recently she'd no idea Walter had such interesting ones. The repeated mention of a particular lady of their acquaintance had been an eye opener, if such an expression could ever be used by a blind woman.

She sighed heavily. Once, she would have meddled or at least discussed the depths of Walter's feelings to ascertain what she might do to help. But without her vision to guide her questions, she didn't dare involve herself. She might embarrass him or make him angry. Imogen couldn't afford to lose his support. Until she had her own future settled, she was utterly dependent on him. She relied on him to keep her informed of any news and provide companionship.

Tomorrow she would apologize and perhaps he would regale her with the latest escapades of their friends. Surely something important had happened today. There was always some to-do to laugh over together.

She eased her bottom onto the top step and pressed her hands together on her lap as she breathed in the crisp warm night. Imogen had always enjoyed the dark as a child. She had never feared what couldn't be seen in the shadows and had slipped from her back door to Abigail Watson's garden gate more times than she could count without concern of being discovered.

These days, Imogen didn't like her chances of making the trip alone without misadventure. It was one thing to not see into the dark night but quite another not to see the dark night at all. She missed quite a lot that went on about her and she was just a bit apprehensive about that. Abigail had once told her she was brave but that was a long time ago. An eternity it seemed.

As she sat in silence, she became aware of footsteps drawing closer. She fumbled up a stair, thudding into the closed door behind her back. The footsteps stopped. A sigh reached her. Male. Deep tones that made her senses tingle. More footsteps sounded until whoever it was stood directly before her at the foot of the stairs. Her pulse pounded so loud she could barely hear her own breath. "Who's there?"

"Hello, Imogen."

She startled, her limbs trembling at the shock of hearing Peter Watson's voice again. Sir Peter Watson. He couldn't have come. She would have heard someone speak of it. Walter surely would have told her if he'd known her former betrothed was living next door again and so would the Perkins'. Her brother wouldn't be so cruel as to keep the news to himself. Or was that why he'd asked after her happiness? Did he fear telling her that Peter was visiting Brighton briefly?

She forced herself to her feet on the step and dipped into a barely passable curtsy in the direction she thought he stood. "Sir Peter."

He sighed loudly again. "Forgive me for disturbing you. I was unable to sleep and saw you sitting there in the dark. I thought I should at least say hello. How are you?" A softly uttered curse left him. "I mean, um, its good to see you again."

Imogen smiled a little sadly. She couldn't really say the same because she couldn't see how he'd changed in the past year. Peter had always been a handsome man, proud in his appearance and neat to a fault. She hadn't minded that streak of vanity in the least. With the funds to secure a London tailor and boot maker, she could only imagine he was turned out splendidly. "It's nice to hear your voice again."

"Please sit down, Imogen."

She imagined him gesturing to the steps beneath her and suppressed a smile. During their engagement he'd been unfailingly polite, never once taking liberties or flirting. That lack of deeper feeling had made it easier to let him go. His heart hadn't been involved in their engagement and it would have been unfair to keep him to their arrangement. She hoped someone special had turned his head while he'd been away. He deserved to be happy.

Imogen eased onto the step cautiously, eager not to fall on her face and embarrass herself before the man she might have married if circumstances had been different. "And how did you leave your sister? Is Abigail still leading Hawke a merry chase?"

"She's so happy it makes one's stomach churn. They both are."

The amusement behind the complaint made her chuckle. "They are definitely in love then."

Peter moved, brushing against her legs as he sat one step lower than her. She inhaled the scent of sandalwood, brandy, and a lingering scent of lilac she wasn't used to, discovering in the process she did not care for the combination in the least. Had he married and brought a wife with him to Brighton? She should be happy but the idea gave her little peace tonight. Not when her own future seemed so bleak.

"I spent the last months sharing the London townhouse with them," he advised. "Quite unsettling the way they carry on still. It's good to be home again and unpacked."

She frowned. Abigail had mentioned none of that in her weekly letters. In fact, now she thought over her correspondence, Abigail had barely mentioned Peter at all. "You're not going to live in London or at your estate?"

"That's right," he grumbled. "Why does everyone seem surprised I prefer Brighton to London or Hereford?"

"Well, you are a landowner now, or so I recall you telling me you would be." As her eyesight had failed, Imogen was left to her memories and imagination more and more for a source of entertainment. Picturing Peter, a man who never cared for muddy boots, striding through cultivated fields had proved an amusing remedy when her spirits were low.

Another deep sigh and his boots scraped on the steps. "Your brother didn't tell you I'd come home today, did he?"

"No." She wrinkled her nose. It itched. Now that Peter was sitting at close range, the scent of lilac was growing annoying. "He didn't tell me anything at all tonight. I did think him quieter than usual."

"Humph," he grumbled. "I sold the property. Took one look at it and ran back to London. It sold for a tidy sum."

What had he been thinking? He had a position, an estate that would have proven an asset to his family's future. Maybe he sold it to appease his wife. Did he love her so much that he acted irrationally? The idea unsettled her more than it should but she pushed her concerns for his home life aside. "So you have fewer responsibilities."

He bumped against her legs briefly. "I'm sure you would have realized long before I did I'm definitely not suited to land management. The dashed property was so far away from the ocean I couldn't possibly stand to be there above a few days. Even London is too far away from the sea. I leased the townhouse to Hawke and my sister and was very happy to leave all that nonsense behind."

Despite her concerns about the choices he'd made, she smiled at the image he'd just painted. She'd honestly thought Peter would have preferred London. The capital was always busy. He could have spent many a night gambling away his fortune in one hell or another. With luck, his wife loved him enough to prevent him indulging in excess in that vice. The right woman should make him happy. But Imogen did wish she sprinkled less perfume near Peter. Her eyes watered and she dabbed at them.

"What will you do with your time now?"

Peter sniffed and then fabric rustled, a heavy thump sounded some distance away and the scent of lilac vanished. "Hmm, would you believe I returned to berate my favorite author for her tardiness in producing a new book?"

Imogen gulped and closed her eyes. Had Peter not been told she'd lost her sight? She had hoped Abigail or Hawke would have mentioned it in passing and spared her the difficulty should they ever meet again. "There's no hope I can write anymore."

He smothered her hand with his and squeezed. "I am so sorry about your sight, Imogen. I had no idea until today. What do the doctors say can be done?"

She laughed bitterly as she soaked up the brief comfort he offered. His touch was quite unexpected but exactly what she needed tonight. She'd been feeling sorrier for herself than usual. Leaving Brighton and her brother, while the right thing to do, would break her heart. "Quite a lot, but mostly the same suggestions. Rest and pray. I don't think it's working."

"Imogen," he began, his thumb stroking her palm. "There's a question I must have answered. When did you suspect your eyesight was failing? Before or after?"

Imogen struggled to focus on his words because what he was doing to her hand stirred delicious sensations through her body. She almost couldn't breathe. "I don't understand."

He gripped her hand tightly, ending the caress. "Before or after us?"

Imogen retrieved her hand and rubbed her damp palm over her gown. "I suspected something was wrong before. I hoped it was merely tiredness. I didn't think it would matter but it grew worse and then you came into the title. I knew I'd placed you in an impossible situation."

His breath caught and then slowly released. He pressed his hand over hers again. "How could a marriage between us have been impossible?"

"A blind wife was too great a burden to inflict on Sir Peter Watson. Besides, none of it matters now."

There was a long pause and utter silence in which Imogen could only imagine the acceptance on Peter's face. Surely he could see the sense of her decision. She'd wanted to spare him the burden Walter now bore. He retreated, pacing away and then returned. She had the sensation he was looking straight into her face. "I'm the same man, but I'm not sure which of us is the more foolish. Did you not think I deserved to know the truth and make my own choice?"

Imogen drew back a little, startled by the agitation underlying his words. "It was the sensible thing to do. You were free of an attachment that would have proved a hindrance to the advancement of your happiness and affections."

Peter began to laugh. The bitter sound cut her to the bone and she winced, wishing he'd never come back to Brighton to remind her of what she'd given up a year ago. Being near him again and knowing he'd done what she'd wanted all along, found his own happiness, made her heart ache. It was as if the day she'd let him go had just happened. "Please," she whispered.

He stopped abruptly. "I should go before we are seen together. Good night, Miss George. Perhaps I'll see you tomorrow."

Not if she could help it. There was no need to meet with him again. She just hoped his wife never came to call. She wasn't sure she could bear it. "Yes. Perhaps."

Chapter Seven

Peter stared morosely out at the ocean, watching his friends paddle back and forth in the morning sun with abundant energy. His mood didn't suit the activity. He couldn't get the image of Imogen, as she'd been last night, from his mind. The corners of her eyes still crinkled when she smiled, full lips still parted in surprise at the sound of his voice. But she hadn't seen what he'd become—a man worthy of respect and not an object to pity.

At least now he knew the truth. She had ended their betrothal because of her failing eyesight and her belief that she'd be a burden for a newly title baronet, not because she didn't care for him. She did care. That's why she'd set him free. She didn't understand the first thing about his nature if she believed he'd be better off married to someone else. He had been the lucky one being betrothed to her.

He slumped to the ground and pinched the bridge of his nose. He'd not slept a wink. The discovery of her sacrifice changed everything. He'd come back with a hope of establishing some sort of relationship with her even if it were simple friendship, but overnight he'd discovered he'd nurtured the hope of perhaps making her regret her decision to end their engagement.

But she was blind.

She couldn't see to write.

Curse it all. She had given up everything.

Imogen George was the most maddening woman he'd ever met.

"Good morning," Walter George muttered as he reached for a towel to drape about his hips. His long wet legs stopped nearby, dripping water.

Since their group bathed *sans* clothes, Peter averted his gaze until Imogen's brother was decently covered. When he did look up he was surprised by Walter's appearance. In the last year Walter George had changed. He'd lost that weak, soft look he'd had all his life and grown muscular. Had he lost weight from worry? "I thought we were friends. Why didn't you write to tell me about her?"

Walter shook his head. "I didn't know there was a problem for months after the engagement was broken. She made me promise to keep the discovery private for as long as I possibly could. I was forbidden to even write to Abigail about it, but when she and Hawke came down at New Year's, she couldn't hide it any longer."

Of all the ridiculous things to do. Hiding from her friends was not the Imogen he remembered. She was fearless under normal circumstances, but the loss of her sight had possibly destroyed her confidence. Given her surprise at hearing him speak last night, he concluded she hadn't expected him to return to Brighton ever again. The news wasn't what he wanted to hear and he felt compelled to set the record straight. "I would have come back."

"Why? You were no longer engaged."

He scrubbed a hand through his hair as frustration curled within him. "I might have been able to offer some help. I could have scoured London for a physician skilled in treating eye disorders and sent him to her. There are discoveries made every day that have not reached this place."

Walter threw a shirt over his head, and then sat at Peter's side, staring out at sea. "She's had enough of doctors prodding her. Made me promise not to bring another stranger home with me."

Stubborn wench. "And you're happy with that?"

"Of course I'm not happy. She's my sister and it's difficult to see her as she is. Barely leaves the house. Now that your sister is gone to London her only callers are Miss Radley and Miss Long, when she can slip away from the viper she calls a cousin."

Peter started at the venom in Walter's voice. "What has Miss Merton done?"

Walter's face reddened. "It doesn't matter. She'd just better stay away from my sister in the future."

A discomforting sensation crept over Peter. "Walter. What has Miss Merton done to Imogen?"

"She didn't have to say a word, but she's done more harm than I care think about." He stabbed a finger in the direction of their houses. "I blame her for my sister becoming a recluse and putting ridiculous notions in her head."

Dread curled within him again and he forced himself to calm before he spoke. "Such as?"

"Imogen has asked me to write to Hawke. She wants him to purchase a house with her inheritance, one far away from Brighton, and then she wants me to interview female companions with the intention of hiring one to live with her. She said she didn't want to be a burden for the rest of her life."

Peter sucked in a sharp breath. Imogen planned to disappear completely. First from him and then from everyone else she knew. If he hadn't returned when he had then he might never have seen her again. This had to be stopped. "What progress has Hawke made?"

"None. I'll not allow it. The letter will not be sent."

Peter stared out at the sea as his panic subsided. "Good." Home had always been Brighton, but part of the allure had always been his friends. Imogen was a friend too. If she wouldn't marry him then he could at least try to help her in other ways. She'd pushed him away to spare him the burden of her needs, constant care and attention. To him, that sounded exactly what good friends should do for one another.

But how to convince her to let him help? She'd been rather cool by the end of their discussion. Any closeness he'd imagined by their brief touch had disappeared as quickly as it had come. He nodded to himself. He would help whether Imogen wanted him or not. He would not abandon a friend. He met Walter's gaze steadily. "I'd like your permission to call on your sister and perhaps invite her to stroll along the esplanade or take a carriage ride with me, with a suitable chaperone of course."

Walter's eyebrows shot up. "That will take some doing. I remind you again she doesn't like to leave the house. She's not had a gentleman call on her, besides Radley and Merton and the physicians, in a year. She won't even consider discussing marriage and believe me I've tried. She's always wanted a home of her own. I suppose even without a husband she's planning for that."

Peter gritted his teeth, but he wasn't surprised. Imogen had a definite plan in mind for her life. Escape into obscurity. Peter would not allow it. Becoming Lady Watson might not be part of the future she wanted, but perhaps he could keep her in Brighton, and among friends, with the allure of continuing her writing. He could help. He would be honored to help her in any way he could. "It cannot hurt to try."

Walter started to laugh. "We had a rule once, Peter. To treat each other's sisters as if they were our own. Then Hawke and your sister married and you became engaged to my mine. Do the rules concerning dallying with sisters no longer apply?"

"I'm merely talking about bringing her into the light, nothing more."

"Are you sure?"

Peter dug in the sand with his fingertips. "It doesn't feel right to have abandoned her when my situation improved so drastically. It never felt right."

"Why? Wasn't it Imogen who set you free? She explained the break was through no fault of yours. In all honesty, we expected to read a wedding announcement in the papers that you would marry a duke's daughter or someone of high stature, or hear whispers of your exploits among the less than proper ladies."

Peter's stomach flipped and his mouth grew dry. Is that what Imogen imagined too? That he'd find a replacement for her so quickly. Peter shook his head. "Not really to my tastes. I prefer a little intelligence beneath the pretty face."

"You never bothered with a woman's head before." Walter's eyes widened. "Are you in love with my sister?"

He frowned and looked away, his pulse racing. "I never said that."

"But you must be." Walter touched his shoulder and turned

him back from the view of the sea. "Why else offer assistance to a woman who cast you aside?"

Peter squirmed. For the past year he'd experienced the sensation that he was not whole. Even in the midst of a crowded ballroom the entertainments had fallen flat of his expectations. And despite some rather obvious interest from some of the ladies he'd met, he hadn't once been tempted strongly enough to even kiss one. It surprised him now to discover he'd remained faithful to Imogen. Even if she didn't want him. Even if she'd sent him away with hurtful cold words. No one would understand. "It is the right thing to do."

"Have you spoken with her?"

Peter filled the hole he'd dug and patted the sand flat. "Yes, last night. She was sitting alone in the dark on the rear steps of your home when I left Valentine's and took a stroll around the block."

When Walter started to splutter about impropriety and the dangers of a blind woman stumbling about in the dark, Peter quickly set his mind at rest. "We talked for a short time and I left her sitting on the steps. However, I loitered by the garden gate to be sure she safely returned indoors. She never came to any harm."

Walter cursed. "Damn woman won't come out of the house safely on my arm but ventures into the dark without adequate protection."

"I must admit I was worried too at first which is why I stopped to speak with her. She may have lost her sight but not her reason. She was on the very top step. She could have easily shouted for help if it was needed."

"If she's so headstrong how are you going to convince her to see you? Will you ruin her reputation by cozying up to her in the dark again should your paths cross?"

Although the idea held a certain appeal, he doubted Imogen would allow that sort of thing. "Ruining her isn't my intention. With your permission I'd like to convince her to return to writing. Since I know of her work, and her need for secrecy, I am well suited to the task of assisting her. She must miss it dreadfully." He offered a reassuring smile he hoped would set Walter's mind at ease. He knew what he was doing. Imogen had a talent that was going to waste and if he could help her bring new stories to life, he would gladly give an hour or more every day. "If our interactions harm her reputation you can be assured I will do the right thing. Believe me, I had honorable intentions last year. I played the respectful suitor already so have no fear that I would do anything to harm her reputation and leave her to suffer the consequences alone."

"Did you really play the gentleman?" Walter rubbed his jaw and then his eyes widened. "No wonder she broke it off. Imogen has always said that a careful, passionless relationship is a marriage doomed to fail."

Peter cursed. If only he'd known her views. By being an utter gentleman he'd convinced Imogen he hadn't wanted her. That couldn't be further from the truth and it was time to show her just how badly she'd misjudged his intentions.

Chapter Eight

———◆———

"Sir Peter Watson to see you, miss." The butler's sudden announcement caught Imogen by surprise. She was not ready at all to greet Peter today or any day.

She rubbed her eyes, wishing she'd remained above stairs this morning. "Could you tell him I am otherwise engaged?"

"I'd like to, miss, but he's standing right beside me."

Imogen gulped nervously. It was the height of bad manners to pretend to be busy when a caller came. To be caught at it was far worse.

One set of footsteps came toward her. "Hello Imogen."

Although she strained her senses, she couldn't detect another presence with him. "Sir Peter." She stood quickly, forgetting her lap was full of embroidery yarns she was attempting to straighten as a gift for Teresa Long. "Oh."

Imogen dropped to her knees, running her hands over the thick, carpeted rug in search of them. She gathered them up, and then struggled to reposition herself on her settee. By the time she lifted her face it was hot with embarrassment.

Peter sat at her side. "You missed a couple."

He placed them gently on the palm of her hand and covered them with his.

"Thank you."

Thick tension swirled between them. She wished she could

see. If he pitied her then she could forget how badly his nearness affected her. She could pretend the warmth of his hands hadn't tormented her sleep the night before. When he released her, she could breathe again.

"These are for you." Damp flower stems were pressed into her hands and the bunch guided to her nose so she could inhale them. "I remember you preferred lavender to lilacs and a modest bunch to excess. The flower seller thought my requirements quite amusing."

"The lady on Ship Street corner?"

"The very one."

Imogen buried her nose in the flowers as the simple thrill of receiving a gift made her smile. No one had brought her flowers in quite some time. "Thank you. She always has the freshest flowers."

"I remember. You told me that last summer."

The sound of paper crinkling caught her attention and she lifted her face.

Peter took the flowers from her hands gently. "Mr. Perkins, can you place these in water for your mistress? I promise to behave while you are gone."

Imogen pictured Peter smiling at Mr. Perkins and grinned. Like everyone else she'd met, Perkins was not immune to Sir Peter's charm. When they were engaged to be married they had often been alone in this room. They would trust Sir Peter more now that he was married. He would never disrespect his wife.

She held out the flowers for her butler to take. "Could you place them in the dining room?"

"Yes, miss." Perkins hurried away.

Peter caught up her hand in his and squeezed. "Do you want to hear whatever news is in the paper today? There must be something to amuse."

Imogen jerked her hand back and scrambled to straighten the threads lying in her lap to hide her confusion. Peter should be with his wife, shouldn't he? She inhaled but detected no trace of lilacs about him this morning, just sandalwood and the faintest hint of the sea. The lure of the news proved too much temptation. "If you have the time."

He opened her hand and placed a small weighty parcel on her palm. "These are for you as well. I'm sure you'll recognize them without requiring an explanation."

Imogen passed the small parcel between her hands, noticing a distinct familiarity in the texture and dimensions. She immediately lifted it to her nose and inhaled the scent of caramels. "Are you attempting to sweeten my mood?"

"Is that even a possibility?"

The teasing response took her by surprise. Imogen didn't answer. Peter should be happy to have escaped marriage to a blind woman, but he acted as if the situation and her condition were of no importance. She should have questioned Walter about Peter's life before he had gone out. Peter did not act like a married man yet she couldn't ask him his situation. She wanted to know what was different about the man at her side.

When he shook out the paper and began to read, her heart fluttered. His voice filled the room and smothered her with sensations she fought hard to deny. No one else assumed to do so many little kindnesses when they visited. Peter hadn't rushed to pick up her spilled yarns, treating her like a capable woman rather than an invalid as Walter often did. And he brought precious gifts from the outside world that she'd missed but had forgotten how much. Being blind meant one only discovered what she heard, smelled or touched in her small world. Peter brought the world with him.

Occasionally, Peter asked her opinion on the news he'd read out loud and she hesitantly ventured to voice her views. They discussed politics at length and then he fell silent.

"What's wrong?" she asked at last.

Paper crackled. "The heroine in *The Lady Most Likely*. Did you base her on Miss Pease by chance?"

"I base them on no one in particular. To do so would draw unwanted attention and create difficulties for Walter and myself."

"But," he leaned close enough that his breath caressed her cheek. "I chanced to dine in Miss Pease's company last night at Merton's, and this morning I was struck by certain similarities to the innkeeper's daughter you wrote of. The giggly laugh, the over-application of perfume, and the distinctive way she cut her food into the tiniest of pieces before she loaded her fork. Could two such creatures exist without there being a slight coincidence?"

Imogen blushed at the mistake. Usually she was more discreet in her descriptions. "Well, perhaps one or two character traits might have been drawn from previous meetings between myself and Miss Pease. I do write about the world around me."

"And you will again," he insisted.

Although she yearned for what she'd lost there was no turning back. "No, Sir Peter. The time for writing is long gone."

"Maybe not today, but I fear our time is up for the moment." His breath whispered across her cheek. "I shall bend all my efforts to convince you to write again or die trying. May I call on you tomorrow?"

Although it was foolish to allow her excitement over speaking of the world at large, and writing, to overset her sensible plans, Peter's arrival had filled a void of loneliness that had only grown larger as her sight had dimmed. "I won't be convinced, but if you have no other plans I'd be only to happy to receive you and your family should you chance to call again. Please do not feel obligated."

His breath skimmed her cheek again and then lingering warmth pressed to her skin as he kissed her. But why? When his lips strayed to the corner of her mouth, she caught her breath. Surely he wouldn't attempt to kiss her? "I'll catch you later," he whispered.

She tensed at the way he said catch. Just because she couldn't see didn't mean he could take liberties. If he hadn't been interested enough to kiss her when they were engaged to be married she certainly wouldn't allow kisses when he was married to someone else. She sat stiffly as disappointment filled her. "Goodbye, Sir Peter."

Imogen sensed when he stood and his slow footsteps as he left the room told her he was content to leave. When the front door closed behind him with a solid thud, she sat back, rather stunned. In the past Peter, had never stayed beyond the length of a morning call but it seemed to Imogen he'd lingered considerably longer than was proper. Why would he completely disregard the social conventions? He shouldn't dally with her if he were married. And if he was married, he'd had no reason to call today to renew their acquaintance.

Frustrated by the gap in her knowledge, she popped a caramel into her mouth and savored the sweetness. How kind of Peter to remember what she'd purchased for herself when they'd been engaged. She hadn't realized he'd noticed her sweet tooth. Imogen preferred to maintain her trim figure so she hadn't asked Walter or her housekeeper to replenish her supply in a very long time.

The heavy steps of her butler crossed the threshold. "Miss Teresa Long to see you."

Imogen had barely greeted Teresa when the butler intruded again. "Miss Julia Radley has arrived."

A set of strong feminine arms wrapped around her. Julia. "You survived his call then."

"Whose? Sir Peter's?"

"Well, who else's you silly girl?" Teresa chided in a gentle voice. "I've never seen the man in so foul a temper as he was last night during dinner. When he beat us to your door this morning, I was half afraid of what he might have said to you. It was very clear to all last night he hadn't known of your situation and wasn't the least happy about being kept in the dark."

Imogen gestured to the chairs around her. "Oh, do sit and be calm. There was no need for him to know. I was the one to set him free, if you recall. What do you think of his wife? Is she very beautiful?"

A vast silence settled on the room and then Julia cleared her throat. "He has no wife with him. He's not a married man, Imogen."

Imogen frowned. Then whose scent was Peter drenched in last night and how had he come to be that way? Had he spoken to her after he'd been with a ladybird? The idea turned her stomach. And if that was the case, she didn't know what to think of his behavior this morning. "I don't understand."

Julia sighed heavily. "Are you sure breaking your engagement was the right decision? After all, you did make a very fine looking pair. According to Linus, Sir Peter spent the better part of half an hour choosing the perfect bunch of scented flowers to bring you this morning after their swim."

"And sweets," Teresa chimed in. "I thought that very thoughtful of him."

Imogen couldn't help the smile that crossed her lips. When they'd been engaged, Peter had been everything that was charming and kind. At least that part of his personality had survived his elevation in rank. "I have to admit that without my sight, pretty flowers without scent fall a little flat as a gift for me. I appreciate his forethought in choosing a scented bunch, and the caramels, but it doesn't change anything. I'd make a completely unsuitable wife for him. Now, tell me what else happened at the dinner last night."

There was another long pause before Teresa spoke. "I know you claim your heart uninvolved, but I must warn you the whole of Brighton will surely have set their sights on Sir Peter as a candidate to marry. Even Melanie."

Imogen squeezed her hands together, disappointment filling her. At least by being blind she'd be spared watching any courtship. "That was to be expected. A titled gentleman is much sought after as a husband."

Teresa patted her hands. "I think chances are slim Sir Peter will be in a rush for matrimony. He's had ample opportunity in distant fields and is still unwed. But Melanie and even Miss Pease looked him over last night as if he were made of gold. I can only conclude that Melanie will add him to her list of candidates for her hand and Miss Pease will become a frequent caller to Cavendish Place in the hope of running into him."

Julia giggled. "I do hope Miss Pease leaves off her perfume the next time Sir Peter sees her. The scent she'd drenched herself in made his eyes water and set him to sneezing. Lilac. The poor man suffered."

Well, that explained where the scent that clung about his person came from but not how. If he'd only dined with her, he must have seen her again that night. Had he escorted her home and … well, she didn't want to picture anything further.

"That was very kind of you to draw him toward the open doorway for fresher air, though Melanie thought you shamelessly forward," Teresa warned in a low voice.

"Nonsense." Julia caught up Imogen's hand. "I was only doing what Imogen would have done should she have been present. I could not abandon him while his defenses were down."

Imogen shook her head. "You make it sound as if you are at war, Julia."

"Life is war. Have you forgotten what it is like to be pursued for your connections or your dowry alone? Imagine Sir Peter's appeal now. Rich, titled, available."

Imogen laughed. "No, I've not forgotten, but what happens to him is his business and not mine."

Julia released her hand. "Then Melanie will consult her list, judge him the most worthy, and win by fair means or foul so she may shove her title in our faces. You know what she's like."

"Does Melanie really have a list?" Imogen tried valiantly to shake off her distress at Peter married to Melanie Merton. Last year Abigail had plotted to make Melanie Peter's wife but Imogen hadn't believed it a good match then and still didn't. Melanie might be well dowered, but she wasn't kind. She would make his life a misery and last year, Imogen's proposal had spared him the connection. This time though, Peter was on his own. Worry seized her and she clenched her hands together. "Who else is on the list? Anyone we know?"

"Mr. Radley is on it," Teresa said quickly.

Julia groaned. "My brother had better not fall prey to her fraudulent charms. Imagine what my life would be reduced to if we were related. Oh, the horror."

For a moment, Imogen considered asking where Walter might be on the list but then she discarded that thought. Melanie would never have considered Walter. Her brother was safe. "Do you think Mr. Radley might be interested in Melanie?"

"Who knows with Linus," Julia grumbled. "He keeps his interests very close to his chest. I've never detected one kind thought he's had for a woman. We are not close siblings."

Imogen sat up straight, distressed by what she was hearing but unable to take part fully in the discussion because she could hear one thing and miss the expression that went with it. Julia could be making fun for all she knew. Imogen really didn't know much of what went on between her neighbors anymore. "Well, let's hope Mr. Radley has enough sense to avoid her snares and traps."

"Let us also hope Sir Peter will do the same," Julia added, "and remembers where his best chance of happiness lies."

"Sir Peter will make the right choice without any interference," Imogen replied quickly. She had to stop her friends from plotting her second engagement to Peter. He deserved a wife who could be his equal in all things rather than a millstone about his neck.

Chapter Nine

Women, wine and wagers. That was usually the topic of conversation when Peter and his friends played cards. The comfort he found in the gathering settled his decision to return to Brighton and leave greater society behind. This was as near to content as he'd ever been in the last year. He helped himself to one last forkful of chicken and then resumed his seat at the head of his dining room table to place his modest bet.

"Friday night has not been the same without your presence, Sir Peter. Always a handsome spread." Walter George confided from behind a plate piled high from the contents of the sideboard. Despite his slimmer profile it was clear his appetite had not been reduced as he plunked a second helping at his end of the table before digging in with gusto.

Friday night had been the highlight of the week in his household in previous years. At that time, he'd needed to keep up appearances so no one would ever know how close to the wind he'd sailed. He shuddered at the thought of debtor's prison. If not for Imogen offering him a life raft, that in the end he hadn't needed to cling to, he'd have already been there and miserable, but then fate had swept him into a greater fortune than he'd ever dreamed. Yet over the past year he'd been far from content. He could afford to gamble as much as he wanted now but strangely found he wasn't so keen to risk the security of the funds.

George belched and tapped at his chest. "Pardon me. My stomach has missed you."

Peter laughed. Walter George was rather uncharacteristically cut this evening. His cheeks held a cheerful ruddy glow brighter than a burn on a summer's day. Given what Peter knew of the stress of life with Imogen as she was now, he judged Walter George probably needed to take his mind off his troubles for one night.

Peter tossed a few coins onto the growing pile and picked up his cards again. "I'm in."

The others cheered as Radley matched his bet. "We've all missed Friday night cards here," Radley confided. "How else can we get a moment's peace away from our families?"

Merton chuckled softly. "Is Miss Julia causing you trouble again?"

"If only I were sure of that." Radley frowned at his cards. "I swear the way she's smiling she's got a secret admirer."

"Now that is news." Merton pursed his lips as he stared at his cards. "Any idea who?"

"None. The bastard is fast on his feet." Radley stared across the table. "When you called on me yesterday did you notice anyone in the parlor with m'sister as you were leaving?"

"None at all. She was alone when I passed the doorway." Merton folded and sat back.

Radley grunted. "Well, she bears watching. The way she goes on, daring us all to race her left and right, she'll ruin her own reputation without help."

Merton swiveled on his chair to face Peter. "Now do tell us about the ladies you encountered during your time away. Were there none to tempt the new baronet to play?"

Peter laughed at the brash question, aware Walter's gaze had sharpened on him and was no longer indifferent to what he might say. "I did meet one lovely lady, sharp tongue, sharp mind. A pity she was closer to one hundred than my own age."

The table burst into laughter, all but Walter. He stared.

Radley leaned forward. "I know a lot of pretty ladies who'd be only to happy to meet a young and well to-do baronet. You've only to say the word and the world is yours, you know."

Peter smiled at the irony. A year ago he'd been desperate to find a solution to his problems but had been overlooked by all and sundry. Now the title opened many doors for him but none he wanted to walk through. "I'll pass."

"Suit yourself," Radley drained his glass and rose on unsteady feet. "But don't think your title and money will always smooth the way with everyone. More men have been made unhappy by a pretty face without the right connections. You should choose wisely."

He intended to. He remembered Imogen's face as she'd inspected his simple gifts that afternoon. He'd made a good start in renewing their relationship. Her expression when he hadn't stolen a proper kiss had been priceless. He treasured her disappointment that he hadn't taken advantage more than his title or his money. "I think I know what I want and am happy to wait."

Radley's gaze grew sly. "Does Miss George still have you under her spell?"

"I never said that." He quickly emptied his glass to hide the foolish hope that consumed him. He really did wish for another chance with Imogen. He just wasn't sure how to proceed.

"Never denied it either," Radley countered as he set his hat to his head. "Well, I wish you all the luck in the world. She wouldn't even give a friend of mine the time of day two years ago when he went courting her. I'm for bed. Goodnight one and all."

With that Linus Radley scooped up his winnings and weaved his way from the room.

"You've all but declared yourself," Merton remarked as he gathered the cards and slapped the deck on the table.

Walter shook his head. "Don't you think you should wait on my sister to give you some sign your pursuit is wanted?"

"If I waited on Imogen we'd never be married."

Walter's brow rose. "So marriage is your goal after all."

"Yes," Peter confessed. His whole body felt lighter for finally spitting out the truth. He may have set aside his original hopes but the truth was his goal had not changed in the past year. Blind or not, Imogen was the perfect match for him. She was smart, she was witty, and she attracted him. "I just need an opportunity to make her see that her blindness is not the hindrance to a happy and fulfilling life she believes it to be."

"Remember what I told you on your return. She doesn't believe in passionless marriages. You will have to convince her the right way." Walter pursed his lips and then dug in his waistcoat pocket. He glanced at his hand a long moment then slid a key, his front door key judging by the shape, across the polished wood. "Mind if Merton and I continue to play in your absence?"

He gulped at the surprising boon he was being offered. Could it really be that simple to go to Imogen tonight and convince her to give him a second chance to prove he did find her attractive? Very desirable in fact. The idea of having her all to himself was too good an opportunity to pass up. "Not at all. Lock the front door as you leave. I have my key."

He stood, amazed at his luck but ecstatic at the thought of being completely alone with Imogen. When he'd visited with her earlier, her housekeeper and butler had lingered beyond the door making him rather conscious that they were listening in. He didn't think they disapproved; he'd spotted their happy smiles as he'd left. It was just that some things were best kept between himself and Imogen. Peter swiftly left his house, hurried to her door and used Walter's key to let himself into the dark terrace house before he was seen.

As the door closed behind him soundlessly, he hesitated. He should lock the door behind him but then how would Walter return to his own home later that night. In the end, he concluded he had no choice except to leave the door unlatched. He didn't know how long he had to speak with Imogen alone and he shouldn't waste time. He snuck up the staircase hoping any servants would assume he was Walter returning from his evening out. He stopped at the doorway to the bedchamber he believed Imogen rested in and listened carefully. When he heard nothing he set his trembling hand to the door handle and slowly let himself inside.

Chapter Ten

Imogen jerked upright when her door opened and a floorboard creaked with the weight of a footstep. She held still and listened hard. "Who's there? Walter?"

"Hello Imogen."

Peter's voice shocked her and she clutched her sheets against her chest. He shouldn't be in her house at this hour of the night let alone standing at her bedchamber door.

The door closed softly and Imogen's heart really began to thump in panic. "What the devil are you doing in my room?"

His footsteps grew closer. "I wanted to talk to you and since you never go out, I had no choice but to come in."

Imogen wished she could see. It must be close to midnight. "How did you get in the house?"

Metal thudded against wood. "Key."

The sheet tumbled from her hands. "Have you taken leave of your senses? Where's Walter? What have you done? Did you win the key from my brother or stoop to steal it from him?"

"Neither." The bed dipped as he sat at her side. "Lost all interest in gambling when you tossed me aside. Deuced unlucky of me. Would you believe Walter handed over the key to me with his best wishes?"

"No." She swallowed the hard lump lodged in her throat. "He would never do such a thing."

"Wrong. He's not completely under your thumb as you imagine, for which I must say I am extremely grateful. Walter has been surprisingly helpful in my wish to speak with you privately."

A heavy weight settled on her legs. His hand? Imogen fought to breathe as she shook off the sensation she'd lost control of her relationship with Peter. The man she remembered was so lacking in passion he would never dream of risking her reputation. "We've already spoken several times since your return. I've told you we do not suit."

He swept his hand up to her hip and she trembled at the storm of sensations his caress caused in her. She slapped her hand over his, holding his wandering fingers in place.

"If you recall our final conversation a year ago I disagreed." He touched her jaw with his fingertips so lightly she held her breath. "I should have fought harder. When you had no reason to pity me you couldn't get out of the engagement fast enough, discounting any future we might have had together. I gather you wanted a malleable husband and a man with a title and money of his own would never do. The day my inheritance was confirmed you ended us."

She huffed at his claims. "There was hardly any us."

"No." He dropped his hand to her shoulder and skimmed the skin of her neck above her nightgown. "I should apologize for being too much of a gentleman before, I suppose. I never laid more than a finger on you to prove otherwise and I find I regret not being clearer the first time very much."

Imogen clenched her hands together to control her shaking. What had happened to the carefully polite gentleman of last night? "Hardly the behavior of an ardent suitor."

Peter brushed her cheek with his lips. His hot breath fanned over her skin to give her gooseflesh down her arms. "So, it's true you would have had me be wicked and steal a kiss or two before we married?"

Imogen shifted back against the headboard and crossed her arms over her chest. Her breath came in a rush and she couldn't calm it. "If the idea had occurred to you I'm sure you would have done something about it long before now."

His wide palm cupped the side of her head and eased her

toward him. "Imogen, the idea occurred to me. I just didn't want to make a mess of yet another situation. But that was a year ago and I'm no longer a patient man."

As she took her next breath, Peter's lips crashed against hers, tossing her theory he wasn't attracted to her out the window. His arms encased her in warmth. Desire flooded her senses. She struggled to know how to respond as Peter took command of the kiss. He tugged at her lips, the tip of his tongue danced across the tender skin until she gasped.

A groan left him as he slipped his tongue into her mouth and tangled with hers. He pulled her closer, into his arms, freeing her from the barrier of the sheets that stood between them. He cupped her face as he softened the embrace, pressing kisses gentler than she had ever expected to her lips. "Should have done that long ago," he whispered when he drew back momentarily.

The next instant he kissed her fiercely and her limbs turned to butter. She melted and threaded her fingers in his hair, anchoring herself to him so she didn't fall. But she was already falling. Falling straight into a desire she had dreamed about, written about, but never experienced or expected to. Peter. She had not imagined such passion from him. The man was full of surprises. Being alone with him in the dark was more intimate than she'd thought possible.

He released her mouth and kissed along her jaw.

Imogen took a moment to gather her scattered wits. Peter was in her bedchamber making love to her neck as if he had the right to. As if they hadn't spent an entire year apart from each other and were even greater strangers now than a year ago. Never mind his kisses were lovely, so thrilling they made her blush to the soles of her feet. If they were found together her reputation would be ruined. The gossip would be brutal and Peter might feel honor bound to propose to her. She couldn't allow him to sacrifice his freedom just because he might be lonely.

She pushed at his shoulders. "Stop. You must stop."

He drew back. Urgency threaded into his breathing, the pant of it fast over her cheek. "Why must we? It's very clear we both desire each other."

"Because it's wrong."

"Oh, Imogen. Kissing you is the most right thing I've ever done. Accepting the end of our engagement last year was a mistake I don't intend to make again."

She shook her head. The man couldn't mean that. "If it was a mistake then why did you not come back sooner?"

"Because you told me you could never love me and I was fool enough to believe that was the only reason you ended it," he whispered against her neck. "I planned to return the second the title was bestowed, but I confess I was still bitter about how things ended between us. I attended balls and parties, the opera and even a house party or two with new acquaintances. Do you know what I thought at each one? I wondered whether I would have enjoyed them more if I'd had you at my side."

"I wouldn't have seen any of it. My eyesight had failed well before Christmas." A bitter pain pierced her chest. "I woke one morning and couldn't see even my hand when I held it before my face. Poor Walter. I cried for days and he didn't know what to do to comfort me."

Peter kissed her again. "I wish I had been here to comfort you. I would have held you in my arms, wiped away your tears and promised to never leave your side."

It was good to know she hadn't underestimated his character. She'd believed he would stay, would have allowed their marriage to occur out of a sense of responsibility. She knew him well and had made the right decision then as she would now. "That's no life for you, Peter. You deserve so much more."

He shifted on the bed until she lay comfortably over his lap. The position was one she'd never been in before. She felt cosseted and wanted yet free of restraint. He nipped at the skin of her throat. "What I deserve is a lifetime of your kisses and a first look at the next K. D Brahms novel before anyone else."

"If only that were possible." She sighed and arched her neck so Peter could continue if he was inclined. To her delight he devoted several more minutes to her throat before he stopped and simply held her against his chest. This side of Peter she wished she'd experienced when she'd been able to see the passion in his eyes. "I cannot write."

"Yes, you can," he insisted as he settled a warm hand on her waist. The thin barrier of her nightgown proved little impediment to knowing where each one of his finger lay. "I'll be your eyes, fingers, and your willing assistant to do whatever your heart desires."

She froze as his hand drifted along her side, coming to rest below her breast. "I cannot ask that of you."

"You didn't. I offered. The same as you offered your fortune and delightful self to save my worthless hide from debtor's prison. My life is here, Imogen. I've wandered aimlessly for the past year and I want a chance to prove to you we belong together. Your lack of sight makes no difference to the way I feel. Let me prove I can be everything you need."

His mouth descended on her neck again, teasing and setting her senses on fire. His hand rose to cup one breast. She jumped as the overwhelming desire struck her that Peter really did intend to demolish all her false notions of his character. She gasped while his fingers teased her nipple to a hard point through her clothing. For a formerly proper man he was showing a side of himself that was remarkably wicked. She wriggled in his lap. If she was going to stop him from going further then she'd have to speak up soon.

The problem was that his hands were far better than her fantasies had imagined any man could be. She rubbed the soles of her feet on the mattress and the next moment, Peter caught her foot gently and held it still. The touch had her squirming madly. To her surprise, Peter started to laugh softly. "You're so unbelievably sweet."

"No one has ever accused me of that." Imogen tried to free her foot, but he held firm. What a strange thing for Peter to do.

He brushed his lips across hers once more. "Then I'll consider it a secret and tell no one but you."

Her struggles stopped as he began to caress along the outside of her leg, lifting her nightgown far higher than it was supposed to be in the presence of a man not her husband. His fingers teased her knee and then he pressed her knees apart.

The sound of a slamming door on the floor below caught her by surprise and she jerked upright on Peter's lap.

A groan issued from Peter's throat and he buried his face at her neck. "Forgive me for saying this aloud, but your brother is an utter bastard to come home so soon." He wrapped his arms about her body and hugged her tightly. "I have to go."

Imogen turned, rather disappointed by that. "I suspect you should too."

His lips brushed hers, pressing sweet kisses to her lips that hinted he'd rather not leave her at all. "I will be back tomorrow and the next day until you see sense. This time, I'll not give up so easy. Sweet dreams, my lady."

He eased her from his lap, kissed her one last time, before he slipped out of the room and down the stairs. If Peter saw Walter on his way out, she didn't hear a word of their conversation. She couldn't imagine what the pair could say to one another at a time like this. Even Imogen didn't know what to think. She wriggled beneath her bedding and sighed at the situation she found herself in. Peter was mad to want her and to her surprise, she might just be mad enough to want him too.

Chapter Eleven

Peter whistled tunelessly as he took a turn around his back garden. Normally he didn't torture the neighborhood with his whistling but Imogen stood at the window of her room in the sunlight, staring sightlessly out at the Brighton morning. He wanted her to know he was there and could see her. When she smiled, he ceased his noise, his heart tumbling like mad in his chest. She lit up like the brightest ballroom in London when she smiled. He should remember to tell her that.

"She's a brave girl."

Peter glanced at his housekeeper where she foraged in his kitchen garden to his left. "She is."

Mrs. Simpson shook the dirt from the carrots and wiped her hands on a bit of rag. "Clear broke our hearts to see her suffering all on her own."

Peter didn't need the reminder. He was well aware he should have been here despite her rebuff last year. "Well, that will change for the better soon. Have no fear."

Her smile turned sly. "Always thought you fancied her."

Mrs. Simpson was far too observant. He winked and raised a hand to his lips to silence her then turned on his heel and hurried inside his townhouse to collect his hat and gloves before a startled Mr. Simpson could offer them. "I'll be out for most of the day."

His butler fussed a moment with his new hat flicking away

invisible specks of dust from his brim and then sighed contentedly. "Very good, Sir Peter. Do you need a carriage ordered?"

Peter grinned. Simpson would soon discover he preferred things to be as they were before he inherited the title. It was a relief to be able to enjoy the slower pace of life at Brighton. "Not today."

He stepped out his front door, traversed the short distance to the George's residence and rapped on the wood. The door jerked open quickly. "Good Morning, Sir Peter."

"Morning Perkins." Peter stepped over the threshold and removed his hat. "I'm here to see Mr. George if he has risen for the day."

The butler gestured to the front room.

"Mr. George could have used a few minutes more of peace," Walter grumbled from his study where he had one ear pressed to the wall. "The strangest noise from your house is driving me mad. An infernal whistling that comes and goes."

Peter winced. "Ah, that might have been me."

Walter looked at him curiously. "You don't normally whistle, do you?"

He grinned, unable to contain the happiness that had gripped him on waking. If he could sing with any tone at all, he'd probably be doing that instead. "Not really."

"Good." Walter put his finger in his ear and jiggled it about. "Damned annoying sound. What did you want to see me about?"

Peter checked that the butler had gone about his business before he replied. "I wanted to see your sister actually. I thought, for propriety's sake I should pretend to be visiting you rather than her."

Walter appeared skeptical. "It won't take long for everyone to guess the truth."

"Hopefully by then I'll have convinced Imogen of the myriad advantages of renewing and deepening our acquaintance."

Walter's face pinked. "I thought that was what last night was for."

Last night had been interrupted before he had obtained Imogen's agreement. What he did know was that her lips and body were made for him. "Sadly, negotiations may take a bit more time than one night. I was hoping to continue my quest today."

Walter's frown grew. "And what will you do today that… ah… couldn't be done last night?"

Peter grinned. "Today, K. D. Brahms lives again."

A relieved smile passed over Walter's face as he dropped to the chair behind his desk and rubbed a hand over his head. "You're happy now to have her write. I thought you disapproved in the beginning."

"I'll admit, I was stunned on first discovery. But I re-read every book she wrote while I was away and I'm utterly astounded by her gift. I'm surprised she hasn't run mad because she cannot continue her storytelling."

Walter winced. "It was a close thing for a while there. In the end, I took her writing table into another room and locked it away. Without the desk to linger beside, she seemed less agitated."

Poor darling. If his plan went the way he hoped, Imogen would have one less reason to be unhappy. She could find comfort in having an outlet for her creative talents. The fact that he would secure a first look at her work was a minor inducement to press on with his plans. And there was always the delightful prospect of a chance to steal another kiss or two. "Can you show me where her writing table is?"

"Of course." Walter smacked the tabletop as he stood. "Come, we'll collect Imogen on the way and break her out of her doldrums."

Walter thumped up the staircase and Peter followed close behind. He couldn't imagine the difficulty he would have faced if he'd attempted to see Imogen like this without Walter's approval and support. After last night's kisses and touches he was eager for more. He couldn't believe he'd walked away a year ago without attempting to claim one single kiss. What an utter fool he'd been. If he had tried and succeeded then, he might not be in the position of having to woo the bride he'd almost had.

As he gained the top step, Imogen stepped out of her bedroom, walking stick in hand, her sightless gaze skimming the hall before her. Today she wore a pretty gown of pale blue. The color made her skin glow but the frown forming on her face dimmed his hopes for an easy discussion. "Who is with you Walter?"

Peter smiled that she could detect her brother's steps without George saying a word. One day, if luck were with him, she would know his steps just as well or better. "Good morning Imogen."

Her perfect mouth formed a perfect 'o' as he drew closer. Her gaze rose until it seemed she could see him. She couldn't, of course, but if he didn't know better he could swear she pinpointed exactly where his face was located. When Walter turned away to unlock the other room, Peter touched Imogen's cheek softly and bent his head to steal a kiss.

"Good morning." Her voice was as breathless as he felt himself to be.

He caught her fingers in his and squeezed. "It's a lovely day out. Would you care to take a stroll along Marine Parade?"

Her chin dropped a little, and worry added creases to her forehead. "I'd rather not go out."

So, no public wooing. He grinned at the remaining possibility of how he could spend the upcoming hours. "Very well. We'll do something else together."

"Peter, you shouldn't be here." A heavy bang and muttered curse reached them from the other room and Imogen turned toward the sound. "What is Walter doing?"

Peter placed his hands on her shoulders and steered her into the room. "Time to write."

Walter opened the drapes wide, revealing a furnished bedchamber containing the fabled writing desk, a chair and a narrow bed at one end of the room. The other end was piled high with discarded furnishings, some of which he remembered seeing in other parts of the house before. Walter repositioned a small table closer to the furniture, setting a boundary to their work area, and wandered back out with a grin on his face.

Peter let his gaze linger on the bed a moment. If the writing went well, perhaps he could engage in other pleasant activities with her, too. He studied Imogen. Her hands were clenched around her walking stick as if she were uncertain of her surroundings. "Relax."

Imogen glared in the direction of the door. "Does he not care that we are alone. What have you done to convince Walter to behave like this?"

Peter opened the desk, spied quill and ink bottle, a short stack of blank papers and drew them out onto the worktable. The ink swirled inside the bottle when he tested it was still good to use. "Nothing except suggest I might be able to make you happier than you have been. Are you ready?"

"Ready?"

He looked at her but then realized that of course she may not understand his intentions were serious. Her writing was important, and not just to her. "Yes, ready to write. Ready to tell me a story I can write down. How do you come up with your tales anyway? I always meant to ask."

She rubbed her brow. "It isn't easy to explain. No two days ever start out the same, but usually I begin the day thinking of what I want to write and then I sit and compose until there are no more words."

Peter smiled and dipped his quill into the inkpot, ready to take down her words. He couldn't wait to see what she would come up with. "That sounds easy enough."

At Imogen's silence, he glanced over his shoulder.

She stood where he'd left her, fingers still tightly clenched about the walking stick, her teeth worrying her lower lip.

"Imogen?"

"I have no words yet."

"Good, because I need more than one kiss to start my day." Peter tossed the quill away, headed for the door, and quietly pushed it closed. He tugged Imogen into his arms, taking the walking stick from her hands and setting it aside. He inhaled the subtle perfume that clung to her skin. Lavender and another scent he couldn't place. Not a trace of fragrance that would make him sneeze. Then he remembered being with Imogen had always improved his mood.

He brushed his lips against hers softly, marveling he had the chance he should have taken long ago to prove he was a man of passion. Imogen sighed once and then she kissed him back, mouth molding to his, delightful body pressing closer.

He explored her delicious curves slowly with his hands, unwilling to rush even though his pulse raced with excitement. He couldn't wait to touch her bare skin and looked forward to the day when she would be his wife. The passion he sensed in her last night had exceeded his wildest dreams. They would be happy together if she'd just concede that he was right. They needed each other.

Suddenly, Imogen pushed hard against his chest until he released her. Although her face was flushed and her chest rose and fell quickly, she merely stared at his waistcoat with a determined expression on her face and said nothing to him.

Alarmed by her sudden withdrawal, Peter scrambled to apologize. "I'm sorry. What did I do wrong?"

"Nothing," she said and then rose on her toes, caught him about the neck to pull him close again. She kissed him soundly. "You did something incredibly right. Quickly, write this down exactly as I say it."

Peter spun back to the desk, adjusting the bulge in his trousers before he sat and cursed the end of his exploration. He dipped the nib in the inkpot and quickly scratched out what Imogen said next. She paced behind him and spoke at a speed that he could write to but an hour later, when she'd not paused for longer than a breath, he begged a halt. He threw the quill away and flexed his fingers. "My hand hurts like the very devil itself."

She drew close behind him and caressed his shoulders, sending goose flesh racing all over his body. "Forgive me. Did you manage to write any of it down?"

He looked up at her and admired the contented smile lingering on her face. "I believe I caught every word. Not exactly neat but still legible."

Her fingers slipped forward and caressed his cheek tentatively. "I'm surprised that worked so well."

Even as his desire soared again, set free by her exploration, a thought occurred to him. "You could have hired a secretary long before this."

Her hands twisted into the hair at his nape. "I doubt I could have found the courage to let a stranger hear such terrible words."

Although he didn't mind Imogen touching him in the least, Peter shoved back his chair and pulled her into his lap so he could touch her too. "I was captivated. I have a hundred questions about the heroine already."

She laughed and her fingers rose to his face again, covering his lips. "No questions yet. Save them until the end."

"As you wish but keeping my curiosity at bay will likely prove difficult."

Her fingers danced lightly over his sideburns and the edge of his ear. "That was the roughest of drafts. Later, when each sentence has been polished to brightness, it will be a work to be proud of."

He kissed the tip of her nose and then her cheek. "I'm proud of you now."

She wriggled, innocently brushing her hip against his hardening length. "Shall we give your poor hand a break?"

"Thank you." He looked longingly at the bed and then the door where he was startled to find Walter standing, one eyebrow raised in question. He nodded and Walter went away. Since a romp between the sheets sadly could not be accomplished he'd have to settle for kissing her instead. He wasn't entirely disappointed. Peter caught her lips gently with his and kissed her urgently before Walter came back to check on them again.

Chapter Twelve

Imogen gripped Walter's arm, aware that unknown persons surrounded them and that she could appear clumsy if she didn't pay strict attention to where she placed her feet. The day was warm, a light breeze blew in from the sea, but she could not concentrate on enjoying the outing for Walter was not always the best of guides. "Promise you will not abandon me today," she demanded

Walter sighed loudly, his arm tensing beneath hers. "I've already promised you my full attention for the duration of the outing. What more do you want from me?"

She tightened her grip further and leaned toward him. "Leaving me alone with Sir Peter so often this week is a sign of absolute neglect for my reputation."

"Are you still annoyed over that?" Walter patted her hand. "He seems to have the making of a devoted secretary. Where's the impropriety in the business arrangement we struck?"

Imogen snorted. "Business arrangements are not conducted in that fashion."

"There is all kinds of business. At least he's been honest." Walter chuckled. "He wanted to court you publicly, but you've refused him every opportunity to be a gentlemen and escort you about. Don't deny it. I have ears, too. However, as I recall, you don't really approve of proper gentlemen as suitors. Forgive me if

I place little weight on your complaints. To make you both happy the rules must be bent in the short term."

She snorted again. "Bent? How about completely broken?"

Walter paused. "Then you'd better marry him this time and be done with your protests that a closer association won't work between you. It's apparent to even a blind man you are not indifferent to his attentions. And from what I can see, he is equally smitten with you."

And there was the rub. She wasn't suitable to be his wife, but Peter was unbelievably good company. "I do like him."

"Then marry the man and put him out of his misery before some other woman gets between you."

That didn't appeal to her but still... "It's not that simple, Walter."

"Sure it is," he said immediately, amusement lightening his tone. "He asks. You accept. You move next door and live happily ever after. That's what you've written in your books many times. Are you claiming the rules of attraction don't apply to you?"

Imogen crossed her cane before them and tapped him on the shins with it. "How would you like me to ask when you are going to marry?"

Her brother spluttered. "Never."

"Why not? Are you afraid?"

"Damn right I am afraid. Every woman I've ever met wants nothing more than to change a man into her personal lapdog. That's not the life for me. I'd rather die an old bachelor than have to bend to fit the mold a woman expected."

Imogen bit her lip. "If you think women always try to change men then why are you suggesting I marry your friend?"

"You and Peter are an exception. You're alike in many ways. Stubborn. Bookish. Always have been." He bumped into her side. "I kept an eye on you both at work yesterday. Each time I poked my head through the door you had Peter's complete attention. I know he didn't see me because he didn't pause in kissing you."

"I didn't hear you on the stairs."

A deep laugh sounded beside her. "Miss Radley is not the only one who attempts to sneak around you. He makes you happy, sister. You may not have figured affection or even love into your decision to marry him last year, but I think he has your heart now. Why fight against it?"

Imogen considered that as Walter led her on in silence. To her right the relentless roar of the sea muted the growing murmur of many voices. Walter stopped frequently, pausing to speak with mutual acquaintances and the odd stranger's voice Imogen couldn't place. As usual, Walter neglected to introduce her to some, but she didn't mind so much today. She had a lot to think on. Had she underestimated Peter badly? He said she should have given him a chance last year. In truth, Imogen had been afraid he'd not return and leave her dangling so she'd acted first to save herself from the eventual disappointment. She'd never dreamed he'd come back.

"I say, what a peculiar day to see Miss George out in the sunshine." The vicar's booming voice cut into Imogen's introspection, forcing her attention back to the present and her location on a crowded beach she couldn't see the beauty of.

She lifted her chin. "I'm here for the race, sir."

"But she cannot see it." His daughter, Miss Pease, advised in a perplexed voice.

Imogen inhaled and the scent of lilac swept over her. She blinked her watering eyes and tried not to pull a face at the stench of Miss Pease's distinctive perfume in the air.

"Yes, yes. Quite a wasted effort," Vicar Pease agreed in a loud voice. "Shouldn't she be sitting down, Mr. George, and resting in the shade?"

"I'm fine." Imogen said through gritted teeth. Being spoken of as if she wasn't there was rude, being spoken of in a louder than normal voice set her teeth on edge. She was blind not stone deaf. "Miss Radley will see I have come along to support her endeavors and that is all that matters."

Silence descended. "A word, Mr. George," the vicar barked.

Walter slowly unraveled Imogen's arm from his. "I'd better see what he wants. Stay right here and I'll be back before you know it."

Imogen hated that Walter never stood up to the vicar when he used that tone. Walter had his own mind and often enforced his will, however, the vicar was another kettle of fish. "Walter, you promised."

He patted her shoulder. "You'll be fine. Miss Pease is right here to keep you company."

Imogen hoped she did not roll her eyes at the idea of having a scatterbrained twit watching over a blind woman. It was better than no escort at all. Imogen held out her hand, hoping to encounter Miss Pease's support. When no touch came, she cleared her throat. "Miss Pease?"

Silence. Imogen took a cautious sniff of the air. Not a trace of lilac. She listened but could not hear Walter's voice or the vicar's booming baritone. In fact, it seemed as if the crowd was moving away from her. What was she to do now? Miss Pease had likely deserted her the moment Walter's back was turned and she stood alone with no idea in which direction he had gone. Her palms grew damp inside her gloves. Her worst nightmare had come to pass.

Chapter Thirteen

———— ◆ ————

Peter tapped on the Georges' front door, frustrated that he was running late. It wasn't his fault exactly. He'd overslept and then his housekeeper had decided he needed a much bigger first meal of the day than usual. She'd gone to so much trouble on his behalf he hadn't had the heart not to at least sample every dish. He pressed a hand to his stomach. He'd have to stop her from doing that again. If he ate in such a grand fashion too often he'd never fit his clothes.

Perkins eventually opened the front door.

"I'm here to see Miss George."

"I'm sorry, Sir Peter," Perkins frowned. "Mr. George and Miss Imogen are already en route to the gathering by the sea. You have missed them by a quarter hour."

"Damn. Thank you, Perkins." Peter firmed his hat on his head and set off down Cavendish Place. Imogen wasn't aware he had intended to join them at the race. He'd hoped to surprise her and linger in her company. Then, when the race was over, Peter had a plan in mind to steal her away from Walter and propose at the exact spot she had proposed to him a year ago.

As he turned onto the next street, he ran into Miss Pease and the vicar coming from the direction of the beach. "Ah, Sir Peter Watson. As I live and breathe. My daughter and I were just discussing hosting a dinner in your honor next week. Jane has spoken of you very warmly and I'm sure you must feel the same."

Peter scowled. "Is that so?"

"Why yes, of course," the vicar went on. "'Tis difficult, given the subject of our last conversation, to declare one's feelings so soon, but I am sure that can be forgotten."

The last time he had spoken to the vicar was to advise him that Imogen wouldn't be marrying him. At the time, Peter had been a touch harsh in his tone, but his feelings hadn't changed in any way.

He wanted to marry Imogen.

"Sir Peter!"

Peter turned at the sound of Valentine Merton's voice and found his friend rushing toward him, his arms full.

"I need you," Merton insisted, tossing several wrapped parcels into his arms and dragging him away from Vicar Pease and his daughter at speed. "We're late."

"I know." Peter glanced down at the parcels in his arms. "What is all this."

"A monstrosity. Please don't laugh too hard when you see me in it?"

"Merton, what the devil are you banging on about?"

"I'm the one racing against Julia Radley today."

Peter stopped in his tracks. "Are you out of your mind? I thought she must have convinced her brother to race her and he was too embarrassed to say."

His friend hooked his arm and dragged him onward, frowning. "Radley is against the competition."

Peter shook his head. "Your sister has also been quite scathing of the whole idea. She has been rather harsh toward Miss Radley on the subject, or so I hear. What does she say now?"

"Melanie has no idea and I'd like to keep it that way until the very last moment. I had to wait for her to leave the house before I could follow. Could you imagine the earache I would have gotten if I'd let slip our plans for the race?"

Peter glanced ahead and saw Merton's sister and cousin just ahead. "She'd be unbearable."

Merton spotted his sister too and jerked Peter behind a slowly moving carriage so they wouldn't be seen, but could still proceed.

"Exactly. When this is over I'm sure she'll complain for at least a week or two solid without pause."

"You could always change your mind."

Merton shook his head decisively. "I won't let Miss Radley down at the last moment and have her be disappointed. She has wanted a chance to prove herself for a long time and this is it."

Peter glanced at his friend and noticed the stubborn set of Merton's jaw. He was committed. "Do you think a lot about Miss Radley's happiness often?"

Merton grinned. "There are worse ladies to be captivated by. I like her energy very much."

Peter gave up all attempts at seriousness and laughed at the trouble Merton was heading into with open eyes. "She'll be the death of you. Linus is always complaining about her antics."

Merton shrugged. "Harmless fun. Nothing more."

"If you say so. However, this might not be so harmless to her reputation."

Merton pointed to a distant bathing machine. "I can change there. Julia will be fine. Will you stand guard and keep everyone away. The race begins at eleven o'clock. I don't want to be seen until the very last moment."

Although Peter was eager to catch up to Imogen, he nodded and checked his pocket watch. "You have only a few minutes you know."

Merton grabbed his arm and ushered him across the open beach. "I know. Shut up and allow me to change."

Merton locked himself inside the little rolling cabin. Peter moved away from the door and scanned the crowd lingering on the pretty stretch of beach between them and the starting line. A goodly crowd had shown up for the sport. More than he imagined for such a scandalous turnout. He hoped they were kind to Miss Radley when she lost. It was only fun and not meant to be taken seriously.

He spotted a few familiar faces ahead but not the one he wanted. He was about to give up when he spied Walter, standing in conversation with Linus Radley. Imogen wasn't with him, but she must be close by. He took a few paces forward and finally saw her, standing alone far away from Walter, hands clutched together at her waist. *Damn Walter.*

He tapped on the bathing chamber wall urgently. "I need to go."

He turned without waiting for an answer and hurried across the coarse sand. He was half way toward her when a boy of about ten ran past Imogen on his way toward the seaside gathering. As the boy bumped into her, she spun and then a dog, likely the boy's pet, knocked her off balance on the uneven, shifting ground.

Imogen wailed as she wind-milled her arms, but it was no use. Time slowed for him as she fell. Her head struck the earth. Peter ran toward her, desperately afraid that she'd come to harm. She lay winded with her eyes squeezed shut as if to hide.

"Imogen." Peter touched her gently and raised her into a sitting position. "Are you all right, sweetheart?"

She groaned and buried her face in her hands. "I am mortally embarrassed."

He surveyed her, checked her head for signs of injury and concluded she would be fine. He breathed a sigh of relief. "Not mortally. We can recover from this. May I help you stand?"

She stuck out one hand. "Please."

The crowd around them began to mutter as he eased her onto her feet and dusted sand from her gloves and arms. Peter scowled at them. "Nothing to see here."

He placed himself between the crowd and Imogen to shield her from further scrutiny. "You look lovely."

"I am surely covered in sand, sir. Everywhere a lady would prefer it should not be."

Peter glanced about and spotted Miss Long approaching. He gestured for her to hurry. "Miss Long. Might we trouble you for assistance?"

Miss Long wrung her hands. "Oh, stars. What can I do?"

Imogen sighed. "Would you take me home?"

"Oh, but the race is about to start," Miss Long protested. She darted a longing gaze at the distant crowd.

"Never mind what she said," Peter advised Miss Long. "I'll see her home myself after the race. But would you be a friend and reassure Miss George, from a lady's point of view, that her appearance is flawless. She does not seem to believe me."

Miss Long chuckled and inspected Imogen's gown carefully. When she was done flicking away sand, she rubbed Imogen's arm. "He told the truth. You look lovely. I have to go. Melanie expects me."

When Miss Long rushed off, Peter curled Imogen's arm about his and pressed his hand over it to reassure himself she was secure on his arm. "There now. Miss George, would you like to get closer to the action? I can see Miss Radley waving madly in this direction."

"I'd like that very much, but do you know where Walter went?"

"Yes, I can see him now." How could Walter have forgotten her? "Later, I'll have words with him about how you came to be alone."

"He left me with Miss Pease. Unfortunately, the responsibility was all too much."

"I expect there was no room left in her head besides planning a dinner party in my honor."

So he had improved his acquaintance with Miss Pease. Imogen tried to withdraw her hand from Peter's grip but he refused to allow it.

"Not planning to attend, I can assure you of that."

Imogen sighed. "Your allergies to lilac can be overcome. I'm sure if you explain, Miss Pease might change her scent to keep you from sneezing."

"There is no reason for her to make any sacrifice on my behalf. My reasons should be all too easy to determine. If I was to dine anywhere, I'd rather it be with you."

"I don't attend dinner parties."

He suspected he knew why, but since she didn't add any further information, he was quick to reassure her. "Did I ask for an invite to a stuffy affair?"

Her brow creased with confusion. "Then how?"

"Later," he whispered. "Lets just enjoy the beautiful day together."

After a few steps, Imogen lifted her face to his. "When Walter couldn't see you in the crowd I expected you to be the one Miss

Radley raced against today."

Peter patted her hand. "Not me. I currently lack the stamina to truly be a competitive opponent."

She faced ahead again. "Can you see whom she is to race against?"

"I don't need to. He's not there."

Imogen's grip on his arm tightened. "So she's been let down. Julia will be so disappointed."

"Never fear, Merton will make an appearance, but at the last possible moment. Something to do with his bathing suit and likely embarrassment. I'm under strict instructions not to laugh."

She gasped. "Valentine Merton? Truly."

"Truly. Surprised me as well." Peter checked to see who was nearby. "I think he might be a touch more interested in your friend than can be attributed to friendly competition."

Imogen nodded and then her face lightened with a true smile. "But that's wonderful. He's the least conventional man she knows."

Peter agreed but was still rather surprised he hadn't considered it before. But their pact to treat their sisters as their own did tend to make a man overlook the obvious choice for a bride. He glanced down at Imogen and realized just how lucky he was to have this second chance. "He does have some rather odd ideas at times but I swear I never detected any partiality to Radley's sister before. Even discussed her having a secret admirer the other night over cards. It was likely Merton who Radley suspected all along and she was smiling over this race."

Imogen nodded enthusiastically. "It would take a special man to appreciate Miss Radley's ambitions for her life. I am very grateful to Merton. He won't grumble like a bad tempered beast should he lose."

"Every woman should have someone like that in their life. Even you, Miss George." Peter bit his tongue to keep his proposal behind his teeth. Now was not the time to blurt out the state of his heart.

Chapter Fourteen

---◆---

At last Imogen felt safe. She leaned a little against Peter, sure now she was in capable hands. She was so glad he had found her that she didn't want to release him. Peter talked, about where they were on the beach, who was nearby, and how far they still had to go even while confiding his opinions. The rush of conversation and the warmth of Peter's nearness were, in truth, making her a little giddy.

A few steps later, Miss Merton's voice cut through the noise of the ocean and crowd very clearly. "I cannot believe Radley would allow such a scandal to take place. He should lock her up before she ruins herself and the family name."

Peter steered Imogen away. "Watch your step. The earth is a little soft here."

"Whom was Miss Merton complaining to?"

"To her cousin. What she doesn't realize is today's race should be interesting. Merton is quite fast when he applies himself fully to a challenge."

"Do you think he will let Julia win?"

"Oh, no. No gentleman in his right mind would do that. It will be a fair race, never fear." They continued to draw closer to the crashing waves. "Here's Miss Radley now."

Peter kept hold of her arm until Julia embraced her. "I so hoped you would come and to be on Sir Peter's arm just makes the occasion even more special."

Imogen ignored her comment and fingered the heavy fabric, a blanket perhaps, she detected had been wrapped around Julia's body. "Are you nervous? What are you wearing? Please tell me you're decently covered."

"Not exactly decent but covered sufficiently for modesty at present."

Imogen licked her lips. "How long until the race begins?"

A whistle blew and Julia embraced her quickly. "Now. Wish me luck."

When emptiness descended on her, she held out her hand. Peter captured it and brought her against his side. The crowd gasped, a few laughed. "They're at the water's edge. Merton appears a little startled by your friend's attire and I must say I do wish he had not refused me the privilege of laughing along with them. Where did he acquire such an outfit? I must ask him when this is over. I'll say this: Miss Radley's bathing costume does not leave much to the imagination. Hopefully, the sight of her shapely long legs won't put him off his game entirely."

Imogen sighed wistfully. "I'd be more afraid his attire was going to have the same affect on her. I'd heard you fellows bathe *sans* clothes in the sea, and although I don't particularly care for that view *en masse* I do wish I could see him today."

"We normally do. But not when there are so many witnesses."

He moved behind her, fingers grazing her hip, breath beating against her ear. He gripped her arms. "Ready for the starting shot?"

Despite the brief warning, the pistol shot caused her to jump. Peter chuckled and rubbed her arm. "They've dived through a wave. Julia is clear first and swimming for the distant boat that marks the turn. Good lord she's quick. Merton better get a move on or he'll be left behind."

Peter kept a running commentary, so good Imogen could almost see Julia sprinting for the distant sail boat. Peter caught her fingers in his when the pair rounded it. "Merton is in the lead. No wait. Damn, they're neck and neck again."

"Yes. Yes. Heaven help us. She's going to beat him back to shore."

Peter's grip tightened and then he hugged her tightly. "She won. She won."

He urged her forward, hands gripping her firmly as she wobbled across the uneven ground. Julia's breathless laughter sounded and suddenly she was enveloped by a pair of wet arms. "I did it. I proved them all wrong," Julia chortled and gasped.

Imogen hugged her friend. She jumped up and down too. "I heard. Peter was good enough to commentate." She awkwardly captured her friend's face to hold her still. "I'm so proud of you but dear, you've wet my gown completely."

Julia giggled and embraced her again. "I'm sorry, but I'm too happy to stop now. Berate me tomorrow."

Julia was suddenly gone, pulled away from her grip, shrieking in protest. Imogen swayed but Peter slipped his hand into hers and squeezed. "Merton is being a good sport about his defeat. Oops. I may have spoken too quickly. He's just tossed Julia onto his shoulder. I think he intends to dunk her back into ocean."

When Imogen turned in that direction, Peter held her back. "She's fine. They're both laughing their heads off."

To her right Miss Merton spoke suddenly, "Well, I've never seen such scandalous behavior. Come along, Teresa. I must write to Father about this. I'm sure you are positively scandalized too, Sir Peter."

"Actually," Peter murmured. "I was just debating challenging Julia myself. I'm usually faster than your brother."

Around them, voices rose to encourage the challenge. The noise was deafening and from all directions and Imogen almost covered her ears. The sensation was extremely disconcerting. Peter slipped her arm securely back through his. His breath whispered across her ear. "Miss Merton's gone, dragging poor Miss Teresa Long with her."

"Poor Teresa. She misses out on so much merriment." Imogen lifted her face. "Would you really challenge Julia to a race?"

"Absolutely." He laughed again. "Miss Radley," he called. "I challenge you to a race in a month's time. Same conditions."

The crowd around them laughed uproariously and Imogen felt a part of everything for the first time in a year of abstinence. The race wouldn't be the same thrilling event without Peter's commentary, but perhaps Valentine Merton could be recruited to assist if she asked nicely. She didn't need to miss everything if she dared to ask for help from the right people.

———◆———

Peter hadn't enjoyed an hour by the sea more than his brief time with Imogen. She had enjoyed herself immensely he thought. Her smile was bright and her eyes had sparkled, even if she couldn't see what happened around them. He'd enjoyed talking to her about the race too. She didn't seem to mind he'd babbled far more than he would normally.

He patted her hand on his arm, content and happier than he'd ever been. This was definitely what he wanted from his life; Imogen on his arm, laughing and talking to their friends. They strolled slowly toward their townhouses, a thinning crowd all about them. Walter was somewhere nearby laughing with Julia Radley and Valentine Merton.

He saw many a happy nod in Imogen's direction. Seeing her out and about had pleased many more people than Imogen would realize. Of course, he would tell her everything when they were alone and convince her she need not shut herself away.

Imogen stopped suddenly and moaned, lifting a hand to cradle her forehead.

Peter bent to peer at her face and found her with her eyes scrunched closed. "What's the matter?"

"A sudden sharp headache." She leaned heavily against him, clutching at his coat. "Perhaps I've been in the sunlight too long."

Peter pressed a hand to her forehead. She was a little warmer than he expected. "Has this happened before?"

"No, but then I've kept to the house a great deal of the time." She moaned again and seemed to buckle.

Peter quickly scooped her up into his arms, ignoring her squawk of protest. "Let me look after you."

For an answer, she turned her face into his shoulder and clutched at him.

Walter hurried up to them. "What the devil is this?"

Peter jostled Imogen in his arms until he had a firm grip. "She fell at the seaside and now has a pain in her head. I thought she'd suffered no harm. We should send for a physician immediately and have her examined. I'll take her home and wait with her until your return." He strode off without waiting to see if Walter agreed with his decision.

Imogen pressed her face against his chest. "The light hurts," she sobbed. "I should never have come out."

Determined not to put her down anywhere but her bed, he kicked at the door with the tip of his boot until her startled butler opened it. "Miss George is ill. Her brother is fetching a physician. Send them straight up as soon as they arrive."

Peter quickly ascended the stairs and deposited Imogen on the bed. He brought her a glass of water when she asked for one and stood back, unsure of what to do next. "Where the hell is that physician?"

Imogen rubbed her eyes. "Oh, don't look so worried. I'm sure the pain will pass."

He'd look as worried as he wanted. Peter stilled. "What did you just say?"

He paced toward her, arrested by her eyes tracking his movements in a way they hadn't done since his return. Could she see him? No, that couldn't be. He must be imagining what he wanted. Walter would have told him if such an outcome was at all possible.

"I said don't look so worried." An expression of wonder crossed her face. "Stop frowning like that."

Peter caught the back of a chair as the idea flared into fierce need. "Can you see me?"

She glanced about the room and then her gaze rested on him again. "Not well. The light hurts my eyes but *I see you.*"

He hurried to the bed and pulled her into his arms. "I did not believe it was possible to be happier than I was today, but I surely am now."

He drew back and cupped her face between his hands. Her gaze flickered over his face. Her fingers rose to brush against his lips, his cheeks, his sideburns. "As handsome as I remember, Sir Peter."

He grinned then and kissed her soundly relieved beyond belief. By some miracle her sight had returned. He just hoped there was nothing else wrong.

When the physician arrived, Peter stood at the rear of the room while the elderly man he knew only by reputation peered into each of her eyes. He waved a lit candle before her and Imogen winced, squeezing her eyes shut against the brightness. The physician sat back suddenly. "You shouldn't get your hopes up."

Disappointment crashed through him. Could it only be a temporary reprieve? Surely seeing again after months of darkness was a good sign. "What could have caused the change?"

The elder man shrugged. "Time perhaps or an elevation of the patient's spirits, I cannot say which. The important thing is not to hope for too much more of an improvement."

Peter turned his gaze to Imogen. Worry had creased her brow. He pushed off from the wall, reached her side, then took her hand in his. "We will take whatever good fortune comes from this. Thank you for your time, sir."

The man nodded, his expression thoughtful as he withdrew.

Julia Radley pushed into the room, her clothing slightly mussed as if she'd dressed in a rush. She stopped at the foot of the bed and stared at Imogen, wringing her hands. "What happened? Did I hurt her with all my jumping about? Oh, I'll never forgive myself if I'm the cause of this. It's all my fault."

"I'm all right, Julia. Really. The headache is fading although this room seems terribly bright even with the drapes nearly fully closed."

Valentine Merton, who'd been silently observing proceedings from the hall, stepped up to Julia and curled an arm about shoulders. He pulled her against his side. "I'm sure you did nothing wrong. Come. I think Imogen should rest. George will let us know when we can call again."

When everyone else shuffled out, Imogen tugged on Peter's hand. "Did I really just see Mr. Merton act a trifle too familiar with Julia Radley?"

"You did indeed." He laughed. "I guess his interest is a great deal more fixed than I suspected."

She'd had her sight returned in time to see what might prove to be a most interesting romance. She grinned. "That's wonderful."

"I agree, but imagine what will happen when Melanie finds out." Peter pulled a face. "She'll make Julia's life a living hell."

That was true. Julia had nothing in common with Melanie Merton. She could easily have her feeling bruised. "That's unfortunate."

Peter settled at the side of the bed. "Enough of everyone else. How do you feel?"

She groaned. "Rather silly."

He brushed his fingers across her cheek. "Better silly than sore in the head. Lie back and rest now."

"I don't want to close my eyes. What if…"

She could wake and be blind again.

"Shh." He smiled, and cupped her face, his eyes full of warmth. He pressed a light kiss to her lips. "I'll be here when you wake."

Chapter Fifteen

—— ◆ ——

Imogen opened her eyes to darkness. A scream clawed up from her chest and burst through her lips before she could stop it. She was blind again. The world had gone away. She rolled and buried her face into the pillow as a sob tore free.

"Imogen. Imogen. What's the matter?"

Peter's strong hands rolled her over again and pried her hands from her face. He peered at her in the darkness.

He peered at her.

Imogen threw herself into his arms as her panic receded. It was night, not the dark of blindness that greeted her. She quickly scrubbed away her tears. "I thought I was blind again."

He peeled her from his chest and fumbled at the side table. Light flared and Imogen quickly blinked to adjust her eyes to the brightness. She fell back against the pillows in relief as Walter's tall body squeezed into her room. "Is there a change?"

"It's all right Walter. Just a nightmare."

He moved closer. "You can still see?"

She nodded, tearing up when her brother wiped at his eyes and blew into a handkerchief. "I'll let everyone downstairs know and then send them home until tomorrow."

She shifted into a sitting position and clutched the sheet to her chest. "Who is here?"

"Everyone, except Miss Merton. Watson, would you mind staying with Imogen a while? I think I might go for a walk for some air."

Imogen caught the dark expression on Walter's face before he stumbled off leaving her alone with Peter. Of course Melanie would not come, they had never been friends, but she felt sorry her brother was upset over it.

She turned to her companion, rather pleased he had remained with her through the afternoon and evening. She studied him carefully. His hair was much the same length as a year ago, his coat and waistcoat very finely made but perhaps not so neat as he could have been. "You stayed."

He caressed her cheek, and moved closer. "There's no where else I want to be."

A bubble of happiness welled inside her. After everything she'd done to set him free he was back at her side, wearing a worried frown. She held out her hand and tugged him onto the bed. "People will talk about us."

"Let them." He kissed her lips gently and when he drew back, his eyes were lit with laughter. "It doesn't matter. You've ruined me for anyone else so I'll never make that exalted match you imagined for me."

All she had ever wanted was for Peter to be happy. As she stared at him, she thought he'd never appeared more content. She touched his face. "Marry me."

He grinned. "Must you always be the one to ask? Yes. Of course I'm going to marry you. I'll not let you push me away again. I love you."

She frowned at how quickly he said it. From all she'd heard, men never liked to admit such deep feelings. "Why?"

His expression grew serious. "You were always the one."

Imogen blinked. "You loved me before."

He nodded. "I did, but there is that rule amongst friends not to dabble with each other's sisters. Terrible rule. I suppose I could have overcome it easily enough and gained George's permission, yet I was penniless and I couldn't drag you into hell with me."

She gaped. "You might have told me."

"When we were engaged, I tried to be the perfect gentleman and never let you regret your choice, to prove to you I wasn't a wastrel and deserved your hand in marriage. But you broke it off before I had a chance to show you how greatly I desire to spend every moment of every day in your company."

Imogen brushed away her tears. "You were always so good. I could never understand your gambling."

His smile dimmed. "I stopped going to hells the moment you stood on the beach and told me we should marry. So brave and beautiful. I didn't think I deserved you then."

"And now?"

"Well, I've already decreed myself a fool to let you get away once and I am determined to take every opportunity to never let you regret your faith in me." His smile was blinding.

"I do love you." She looped her arms about his neck. "But what happens if my eyesight fails again?"

"You'll never be alone in the dark. I promise."

He kissed her cheek, her jaw, her lips. When he drew back, Imogen was breathless with desire. Warmth crept over her body at the hot look in Peter's eyes. "Show me what that means."

His eyes widened in surprise when she removed the pin of his cravat, but he did not move to do her bidding or help.

She grinned that she could shock him to silence. The cravat came undone and she slowly pulled it free of his neck. "Lock the door, Peter, and show me what makes us different. I want to see you. All of you."

After a long moment, Peter rolled off the bed and secured the door. When he returned, he was already divesting himself of the clothes covering his upper body. Imogen sat forward, fascinated by the brief glimpse of Peter's skin. When his shirt came off her breath caught. His torso was smoothly muscled with a smattering of hair covering chest and forearms. He was quite breathtaking.

His hands fell to his footwear and finally his trousers sailed across the room. When he was utterly naked, she couldn't breathe. Her imagination had not come close to understanding the power and appeal of the male form. He stepped close enough to the bed that she could reach out and touch him if she was brave enough. Imogen accepted the offer and reached for him.

Smooth, warm, and compelling. Imogen ran her hands over Peter's taunt stomach and heaving chest, drinking in what might be her only memory of his body. She hoped it wasn't, but just in case, she made a thorough examination of every inch within range.

His arms were strong and it explained how he could carry her so effortlessly from the beach. His wide chest narrowed toward his hips and when she lightly skimmed her fingers over his stomach, Peter caught her hands and lifted them away. "My turn."

His fingers wiggled beneath the hem of her nightgown and lifted the material over her head, leaving her utterly bare. He studied her, running one fingertip over her skin but avoiding the places she suspected would be the most sensitive.

Her nipples hardened to pebbled points when he circled them. Her body trembled. Her mouth grew dry. She swallowed. No wonder he'd stopped her exploring him in the same manner. Such light touches were torture. "Peter," she whispered.

He grinned and eased her back onto the mattress. When he settled at her side, he was smiling. "You are the most beautiful woman I have ever met. Both inside and out."

Imogen frowned and rolled to face him. "I wrote that."

"I know. I remembered reading it and it struck me as particularly true." He smoothed his hand over her hip and drew her upper thigh over his. "That is you, Imogen. The most beautiful, lovely and kind person in the world."

Imogen blushed. "You've hardly seen the best of me."

He cupped her rear then drew her body across the bed so she pressed against him tightly. "I want it all. Every moment. Every joy and sorrow. I love you so badly I can hardly think straight."

She touched his face and stared deeply into his eyes, loving the emotions she glimpsed filling them. All for her. He was so confident they belonged together that any reservations fled. If they married and her eyesight failed again, he would not regret the choices he'd made. "Then stop thinking and just love me. Sometimes words can get in the way."

He kissed her fiercely then, opening her mouth with his and sliding his tongue between her lips. Imogen curled an arm about his head and enjoyed the most remarkable sensations he stirred within her as their bodies touched. Restlessness gripped her. She threaded her fingers into his hair and clung to him so he had no chance to get away. He covered her, bringing their bodies even closer. She gripped him and then because he was so warm and close, she slid her hands over the skin of his back. "You feel..."

It was odd not to know how to describe the moment. Her pulse raced, her body craved to be close to him but she couldn't describe the wonder properly. He nodded, staring deeply into her eyes as he widened her legs with his knees. His body fit snugly against her, and excited her beyond reason.

He touched her body with one hand while the other prevented his weight from crushing her. His warmth and gentleness soothed her. "So lovely," he whispered. His fingers drifted lower, over her belly and slid between her legs where she never expected he would want to go. She tensed but the movement only brought a deeper ache. Her legs widened of their own accord as he circled a place that made her cry out.

She clung to Peter. When he moved again, it was to thrust his hips and join with her. She knew what to expect but she still whimpered at the sharp pain that followed.

"Hell," he muttered and froze in place. "I didn't mean to rush like that."

After a moment the pain eased to a dull ache. She met his gaze and saw the confident expression he'd worn replaced by a frown. She slid her hands up and down his back, noting the fine muscles clenching beneath them. "I'm fine."

He cupped her face with a hand. "Are you sure?"

"Don't worry so much. I'm not about to burst into tears."

He smiled then and after a few moments he moved again, flexing his hips just enough to remind her there was no turning back. Imogen slid her hands to his shoulders and he levered up. His thrusts grew faster, deeper until a fine sheen of sweat coated his skin. There was no pain, in fact, there was another sensation building inside her—a slow burn that consumed her every thought. She wanted more. More of Peter. Imogen hooked her legs around his hips and clung.

The change in position doubled her desire. The ache where Peter joined with her grew until she thought she might explode. She met Peter's gaze and bit her lips. She was sure she was going somewhere but she had no idea where. Peter shifted and his fingers tangled between her legs again. Imogen squeezed her eyes shut as she stiffened all over, fighting for breath and strangely escape from her own body. Every nerve in her body shuddered. Every sense stretched then shrank in an instant. She sucked in air desperately as her body slowly relaxed.

After a time she grew aware Peter had stopped moving.

She glanced up quickly. At that moment, Peter groaned, eyes snapping shut as he shuddered and thrust within her a few more times.

Then he collapsed against her, buried his face in the crook of her neck and laughed softly. Imogen didn't think there wasn't anything funny about making love. In fact, it was the most incredible experience she'd ever had. She pushed at his chest until he sat up a bit, still joined with her but able to meet her gaze. "Does something amuse?"

"I used to dream about you." He shook his head. "But I've just discovered, I've a bloody poor imagination. I could never have dreamed up tonight's adventures, my love."

"Surely you've..." she gestured to their nakedness, "...made love before."

He withdrew from her and then pulled her into his arms. "Never. I'm not innocent but believe me you are the only woman I've ever made love to."

She snuggled closer. The idea that there was a difference between intimacy with love, and without intrigued her, but so long as she had the former, Peter's love, she wouldn't worry about who he'd had relations with before. "That is exactly what a woman wants to hear at such a moment."

"Oh no, that's what *my* lady has to believe. Lady Watson. I've always liked the sound of that, you know."

Imogen rubbed her cheek against his chest, discovered the sensations tickled and then stilled. "I suppose I should confess I like it, too."

His grip tightened around her body. "Good. I don't care what happens next, Imogen, as long as you love me and will be my wife. Preferably by the end of the month. I don't think I can count on your brother making himself scarce like he did this afternoon too often before we are married."

She would have to find a way to thank Walter for his support, but not tonight. After an eventful day, Imogen was growing very sleepy. She pulled the sheet over her shoulders with Peter's help. "He's very kind. I don't know what I'd have done without him."

Peter pressed a lingering kiss to her cheek. "Well, you have mine now too for all the days of my life. Rest now. I'll be here when you wake again."

Imogen covered her mouth as she yawned. She snuggled against Peter, her mind at once sleepy and excited for the future. A future she'd never though to have. She'd underestimated Peter in every way possible. Tomorrow, if she could see, she'd pen a new story in secret, one written just for him.

Chapter Sixteen

———◆———

Peter whistled tunelessly as he descended the stairs of Walter George's house. For the first time ever, he felt completely proud of himself. Imogen would be his wife and although he had anticipated their wedding night, he felt utterly justified in being so bad.

There was a chance that Imogen would not see again and he'd not wanted to deprive her of what she'd wanted. That her desires ran in the same direction as his only made the night before so much sweeter.

He stepped into the dinning room and then reared back as a blow connected with his stomach. He gasped for air and struggled to look for his assailant.

Walter George stood before him, a satisfied expression on his face. George glanced at their friends. "Was that sufficient brotherly outrage do you think?"

Merton dragged him upright, ignoring his groan of pain. "He does appear winded and your sister's honor has been satisfied. That should be more than enough for the tattletales."

"I believe it will be, too." Radley's jaw clenched and then he hurried out.

Peter rubbed the ache in his stomach. "What the hell are you doing? I promised I would marry her."

George's smile grew smug. "We never really dispensed with

the rule that made sisters off limits for dalliance. How soon can you get a special license?"

Peter drew a sealed letter from his pocket. "I was about to arrange for this to be sent. I happened to meet the archbishop of Canterbury on several occasions this past year. Nice fellow. Said he'd be very happy to see me wed and get settled. I'm sure I can acquire a license very quickly without having to leave Imogen or Brighton."

"Good." George yelled for Perkins and his letter was taken away to be franked and posted. "I was just about to eat. Are you hungry?"

"Starved." Peter winced as angry color rose in Walter's cheeks. Perhaps that wasn't the wisest choice of words after spending the night in Imogen's bed. However, it was true. He'd missed several meals yesterday due to his concern for her. He followed Walter and Merton into the dining room, and sat where told.

Merton pulled out a chair to his right. "Can she still see this morning?"

"Yes." The memory of her sleepy smile and warm expression caused his heart to thump wildly. "She had returned to sleep by the time I left her so it may be a few hours before she's ready for visitors."

Merton's lips twisted into a smirk that he tried to hide. "I'll let my cousin know. She was most anxious to visit and celebrate the good news of your renewed engagement."

No one could be happier than himself. "I'm very glad to hear Miss Long will support our happy news. What does your sister say?"

Merton's lips pressed together tightly and his gaze darted around the room before he met Peter's. "Best not to say. I'm thinking she should take a trip up to the Lakes district. Mother and Father will be glad to have her home and we have relatives there she hasn't seen in a good long while."

Relatives, but no mention of friends. It would not surprise Peter to know the harpy had none. "Will your cousin go as well?"

Miss Long lived in her cousin's shadow. It would be a shame to have her sent away too. "I think not. Teresa gives me far less trouble than my own sister. She's of a practical, but sentimental, heart and doesn't care to gossip about friends." Valentine shrugged. "Besides, the air here by the sea is better for her health than at the Lakes. It would be cruel to disturb her."

Peter glanced down at his hands. What a bind to be in. He didn't envy Valentine that discussion with Melanie. The girl had a tongue of acid and could speak cruelly of others without a second thought. She would not take kindly to expulsion from Brighton. If Walter hadn't forgiven her for remarks she'd made at Imogen's expense then perhaps it would be better if she spent some time away. Disagreements between friends could end friendships if not resolved and it was worse when family became involved. Having already come close to losing Hawke as a friend, he well knew the damage problems would cause.

Once he and Imogen were married for a while, any gossip about impropriety before their marriage would have run its course and become meaningless. He smiled at the bright future unfolding before him. He felt lighter, more sure than he'd been in years. A home, love and companionship, and complete trust. K.D. Brahms could continue to write fascinating stories in the complete privacy of their home, and he would strive to be everything Imogen needed in a husband. If her sight failed again, they would accommodate the change together.

For when a man's heart was involved, he had no option but to follow where it led when granted a second chance to be with the love of his life.

———————◆———————

Miss Radley's Third Dare

The only person who understood what Julia Radley wanted most in life was the man who accepted her challenge to a bold swimming race, and lost. But when he suggests they marry to quiet the resulting scandal, she discovers the consequences of her actions are far reaching for him too.

About Heather Boyd

---◆---

Determined to escape the Aussie sun on a scorching camping holiday, Heather picked up a pen and notebook from a corner store and started writing her very first novel—Chills. Years later, she is the author of over thirty romances and has no plans to stop. Addicted to all things tech (never again will Heather write a novel longhand) and fascinated by English society of the early 1800's, Heather spends her days getting her characters in and out of trouble and into bed together (if they make it that far). She lives on the edge of beautiful Lake Macquarie, Australia with her trio of mischievous rogues (husband and two sons) along with one rescued cat whose only interest is that she provides him with food on demand.

You can find details of her writing at
www.Heather-Boyd.com